taming the alien

Ken Bruen

BLOODLINES

THE DO-NOT PRESS

A paperback original.

First Published in Great Britain in 1999 by
The Do-Not Press Ltd
16 The Woodlands
London SE13 6TY
www.thedonotpress.co.uk
email: thedonotpress@zoo.co.uk

ISBN 1 899344 49 7

British Library Cataloguing in Publication Data. A catalogue
record for this book is available from the British Library.

b d f h g e c a

Printed and bound in Great Britain by
The Guernsey Press Co Ltd.

For Izzy Bain and Noel Bruen

To Fall
falling
have fallen   in love

Falls knew the guy would hit on her. With such a short mini, it was nigh mandatory. She sat, tasted her drink, waited.

Yeah… here he was.

'Mind if I join you?'

'Not yet.'

He gave a quizzical look. 'Not yet you don't mind, or not yet to joining you?'

Falls shrugged and tried to look at home in the bar. Not easy to carry off when you're:

a) English

b) Female

c) Black.

He sat.

She asked, 'Do you swim?'

'What?'

'It's just that you have a swimmer's shape.'

'Yeah? Well, no… no I don't, not since *Jaws*, anyway.'

She gave a laugh. 'There's no sharks in England.'

He gave a tolerant smile. Nice teeth. Asked, 'How long since you shopped on the Walworth Road?'

She laughed again, thought, Good Lord, if I'm not careful I'll be having me a time.

7

He then proceeded to lay a line of chat on her. Not great or new, but *in there*.

She held up a finger, said, 'Stop.'

'What?'

'Look, you're an attractive man. But you already know that. We'd date, get excited, probably have hot sex.' He nodded, if uncertainly, and she continued. 'I know you'd have a good time – shit, you'd have a wonderful time – and I'd probably like it too. But then the lies, the fights the bitterness… Why bother?'

He thought, then said, 'I like the first part best.'

'Anyway, you're too old.' And it crushed him. One fell swoop and he was out of the ballpark. No stamina and they hadn't even started. It didn't feel good.

'Oh hell,' she thought. 'Revenge is supposed to be sweet.'

Her father, in a rare moment of sobriety, had said: 'If you're planning revenge, dig two graves.'

He sure as Shooters Hill was in one, and she was contemplating the second. All because Eddie Dillon had smashed her heart, her trust into smithereens. The married bastard.

✝

Roy Fenton tasted the tea, went, 'Euck… argh…' and called to the waitress.

'Yo, Sheila, how can you fuck-up a tea bag?'

Sheila didn't answer. The Alien was known in the Walworth Road cafe and most of south-east London. What was known was his reputation, and that said people got hurt round him.

His cousin had been part of the 'E Gang'. A group of vigilantes who'd hanged drug dealers from Brixton lamp-posts until they'd been slaughtered in a crack house on Coldharbour Lane. Smoke that!

No one called Fenton 'The Alien' to his face. At least not

twice. He read his poem, chewed the tea:

UNTITLED
And he had his books,
second-hand
and nearly twenty, neatly stacked
A tape recorder, German made, some
prison posters
Same old ties, some photos too
And the camera, convincing lies.

For the booze
a Snoopy mug,
two shoes too tight
And English jeans
A silly grin with still,
the cheapest jacket
off the rack during some sales.

A belt
its buckle made of tin… and clean
with undies, unmatched songs
and a hangover
God bless the mark
the usual London cover.
A watch
Timex, on plastic strap.

He stopped. Remembering… When Stell had come to the
'Ville, him six months into the three years, and said: 'Ron, I
got pregnant.'

And he didn't know what to say. 'I dunno what to say.'

And she'd begun to weep, him asking, 'What… what's
the matter, darlin'?'

And her head lifting, the eyes awash in grief.

'Ron… I had an abortion.'

9

And he was up. Remembered that. Head-butting the first screw, taking down a second without even trying and then: the clubs, the batons. Raining down on him, like the purest Galway weather. Harsh and unyielding.

Did three months on the block, lost all remission and got an extra year. Not hard time, hate time. Fuelled and driven by a rage that never abated. The head screw, a guy named Potter. Not the worst; in many ways a decent sort. Still some humanity lingering. He gave a hesitant smile, almost put his hand out. No chance.

But tried anyway.

'Give it up Ron, she's not worth it.'

Fenton spat on his tunic.

The other screws moving forward but Potter, waving them back, said, 'Have this one on me, Ron.'

✝

He'd searched every pub in north London. Should have known better than to step outside the south-east in the first place. Jeez... North! Highbury and shite talk.

Word was, she was in San Francisco. OK. He could do that... but he would need a wedge, a real buffer. He was working on it...

During lock-down he'd begun to write the poem. One toilet roll, with a midget William Hill biro. Gouging it down.

One of the nick fortune tellers saying: 'I can see yer future, Ron.'

'Yeah? See a double scotch anytime soon?'

The tier sissy who'd blown him then saw the poem, said, 'You should send that to a magazine.'

Gave him a fist up the side of the head, said, 'Don't touch my stuff.'

But got to thinking...

One lazy Saturday, Millwall were two down, he'd idled through a magazine and these words hit him like a pool cue:

10

If you turned right on the Clapham Road, you could walk along Lorn to the Brixton side.

Few do.

Brant had his new place here. The irony didn't escape him.

Lorn... forlorn.

Oh yeah.

Since he'd been knifed in the back, he'd been assigned to desk duty, said: 'Fuck that for a game of soldiers.'

His day off, he'd go to the cemetery, put flowers on PC Tone's grave. Never missed a week. Each time he'd say, 'Sorry son. I didn't watch for you and the fucks killed you for a pair of pants.'

What a slogan – *Trousers to die for*.

The Band Aid couple had gone to ground or Ireland. No proof it was them. Just a hunch. Some day, yeah... some day he'd track 'em.

Only Chief Inspector Roberts knew of Brant's hand in the murder of the boy. He wouldn't say owt. Brant's own near death had somehow evened it out for Roberts.

Odd barter but hey, they were cops, not brain surgeons.

Chief Inspector Roberts was aging badly. As he shaved, he looked in the mirror, muttered: 'Yer aging badly.'

Deep creases lined his forehead. The once impressive steel grey hair was snow white and long. Clint Eastwood ridges ran down his cheeks. Even Clint tried to hide them. Wincing is cool... sure... maybe till yer dodgy forties, but after that it comes across as bowel trouble.

Roberts loved the sun, nay, worshipped it – and cricket. Too many summers under long hours of UV rays had wreaked havoc. Worse, melanomas had appeared on his chest and legs. When he'd noticed them he gasped, 'What the bloody hell?'

He knew... oh sweet Jesus did he ever... that if them suckers turned black, you were fucked. They turned black.

The doctor said, 'I won't beat around the bush.'

Roberts thought: Oh, do... if necessary, lie to me – lie *big* – beat long around any bush.

'It's skin cancer.'

'F*uck*!'

After he thought, I took it well.

Was ill as a pig when he heard about the treatment.

Like this: 'Once a week we'll have radiation.'

'We? You'll be in there with me?'

The doctor gave a tolerant smile, halfways pity to building smirk, continued: 'Let's see how you progress with the 'rad', and if it's not doing the business we'll switch to laser.'

Roberts wanted to shout, 'Beam me up Scottie! Signpost ahead... The Twilight Zone.'

He let the doctor wind down. 'Later on, we'll whip some of those growths away. A minor surgical procedure.'

'Minor for you, mate.'

The doctor was finished now, probably get in nine holes before ops, said: 'We'll pencil you in for Mondays, and I'd best prepare you for two after effects:

1.   You'll suffer extreme fatigue, so easy does it.
2.   It leaves you parched – a huge thirst is common.'

He had a mega thirst now.

Right after, he went to the Bricklayers. The barman, a balding git with a pony-tail and stained waistcoat, chirped, 'What will it be, Guv?'

14

'Large Dewars, please.'

'Ice... water?'

'What, you don't think I'd have thought of them?'

'Touchy.'

Roberts didn't answer, wondering how the git would respond to *rad*. As if abbreviation could minimise the trauma. Oh would it were so. Dream on.

Robert's other passion was Film Noir of the forties and fifties. Hot to trot. Now, as he nursed the scotch, he tried to find a line of comfort from the movies. What he got was Dick Powell in *Farewell My Lovely*:

> *I caught the blackjack right behind my ear.*
> *A black pool opened up at my feet.*
> *I dived in. It had no bottom.*

Yeah.

He'd given the git behind the bar a tenner, and now he eyed the change. 'Hey buddy, we're a little light here.'

'Wha...? Oh... took one for me. I hate to see anyone drink alone.'

Roberts let it go. Londoners... you gotta love them. Bit later the git leans on the bar, asks, 'You like videos?'

'Excuse me?'

'Fillums, mate. Yer latest blockbuster – see it tonight in the privacy of yer own gaff. Be like 'aving the West End in yer living room.'

'Pirates, you mean.'

'Whoa, John, keep it down, eh?'

Roberts sighed, laid his warrant card on the counter.

'Whoops...'

Roberts put the card away, said, 'I thought in your game you could spot a copper.'

'Usually yeah, but two things threw me.'

'Yeah, what's those then?'

'First, you have manners.'

'And...?'

'You actually paid.'

15

Fenton got his nickname thus: During the movie *Alien*, he killed a guy – the scene where the creature crashes outta John Hurt's chest. He'd used a baseball bat. Near most, it was his weapon of choice. The guy, Bob Harris, had stitched up his mates. They were doing life-plus on the not so sunny Isle of Wight. Mind you, the ferry over had been scenic.
Fenton was offered two large to payback. He did it gratis. What are mates for?

Oh, Bob liked his horror flicks and was a particular aficionado of Ridley Scott's work on *Alien*. Could wax lyrical about the used hardware look of the scenes. Shite talk.

Fenton had called round, six pack of Special and some wacky-backy. They'd done a tote, got munchies and cracked the brewskis. Fenton asked, 'Yo, mate, still got *Alien*, have you?'

'Oh yeah, good one. Wanna see it now?'

'Why wait?'

Indeed.

Fenton said he'd grab some cold ones from the fridge as they got into the flick. Bob was on the couch, glued to the screen, yelping about the 'vision' of Allen Dean Foster. Fenton unzipped the Adidas hold-all and took out the Louisville slugger. It had black tape wound tight on the handle, tight as cruelty. He gave the bat a test swing, and yeah, it gave the familiar whoosh of long and comfortable use.

The crew of *The Nostradome* were sitting down to their meal and John Hurt was getting terminal indigestion.

Bob shouted, 'Yo… Fen! You don't wanna miss this bit!'

Fen came in, put his weight on the ball of his right foot, pivoted, and swung with all he had, saying, 'I won't miss, buddy.'

And wallop – right outta the ball park.

The crew on the TV screen gave shouts of horror and disgust at the carnage. Fenton let the movie run, he hated to leave things unfinished.

✝

Fenton had a meet with Bill in The Greyhound near the Oval. It's always hopping, but no matter how tight, Bill gets to sit on his tod down the end. All the surrounding seats are vacant. Not free but empty, like McDonalds cola. A time back, a pissed Paddy decided to have a seat right up close to Bill, said, 'Howya.'

Bill didn't look, said, 'You don't wanna perch there, pal.'

'Pal? Jaysus, I don't know you. Buy us a double, though.'

A muscle man outta the crowd slammed Paddy's ears in a simultaneous clatter. Then had him up and frog marched out to the alley. There, his arm was broken and his nose moved to the right. After, sitting against the wall, he asked, 'What?... What did I say?'

Bill and Fenton went way back. Lots of cross referenced villainy. Masters of their respective crafts. Bill asked, 'Drink?'

'Rum 'n' coke.'

'Bacardi or...?'

Fen smiled, 'Navy up.'

An old joke. Just not a very good one. Bill was drinking mineral water – Ballygowan Sparkling.

The drinks came and Fen said. 'I dunno Bill, I must be getting old, but I could never get me head round paying for water.'

Bill took a sip and winced. 'What makes you think I pay?'

'Nice one.'

They sat a bit in silence. You could nigh hear the bubbles zip, like pleasant times, like fairy tales.

Then, 'We found her.'

'Great.'

17

'You're not going to like it.'

'Gee, what a surprise.'

'She's in America, like you thought – San Francisco – living with a teacher, name of Davis.'

'A teacher... wow.'

Bill said, 'Let it be, Fen,' and got the look, boundaries being breached. He sighed. 'Sorry... you'll need a wedge.'

'Big time.'

Bill rooted in his jacket, took out a fat manila envelope, said 'There's a cop, name of Brant, needs sorting.'

'When?'

'Soon as.'

'How far in?'

'Not fatal but educational.'

'Can do.'

Fen got up and Bill said, 'Oi, you didn't touch yer rum.'

'Hate that shit.'

And he was gone.

✝

Brant had taken Falls with him to interview a suspected arsonist. No proof had surfaced but the Croydon cops swore he was the man. Now he'd moved to Kennington and, hey, coincidence, a warehouse was gutted on the Walworth Road. He was in his early thirties with the eyes of a small snake. He'd answered his door dressed in a denim shirt, cutoffs, bare feet.

Brant said, 'If you'll pardon the pun, we're the heat.'

The guy smiled, let them know he could be a fun person, asked, 'Got a warrant?'

'Why? You done somefing?'

And everybody smiled. The guy was enjoying it, said, 'What the hell, c'mon in.'

The flat was a shithole. The guy said, 'It's a shithole, right, but I just moved in and...'

18

Brant said, 'From Croydon.'

'Yeah!'

'We heard.'

He stretched out on a sofa, waved his hand. 'Park it wherever.'

Brant parked it right next to the guy's head, still smiling. The guy sat up, decided to pull the 'blokes' routine and nodded towards Falls. 'You didn't need to bring a cunt with yah.'

And got an almighty wallop on the side of his head.

Brant said, 'Here's how it works, boyo – you call her names, I'll wallop you... OK?'

Too stunned to reply, the guy looked at Falls, thus failing to see the second sledgehammer punch to the back of his head. It knocked him out on his face and he whinged, 'I didn't say nuffink that time.'

Brant hunkered down, said 'I hadn't finished explaining the rules. See, if you even *look* like you're going to call her a name, I hammer you. Get it now?'

The guy nodded.

Falls had long since despaired of Brant's methods. She owed him three large for her father's funeral and was obliged to suffer in silence.

When they were leaving, Brant said to the guy, 'They think you're an arsonist. Me?... I dunno, but if there's another fire soon, I'll put you in it.'

Back on the street, Falls said in exasperation, 'I need a holiday.'

'Yeah? Anywhere nice?'

'Some place far, like America.'

'And you need money, is it? How much?'

She was too enraged to answer.

✝

Brant was humming a Mavericks tune as he put his key in the door. He felt fucked and looked forward to a cold one –

19

lots of cold ones – and maybe a sneak peek again at *Beavis And Butthead Do America.*

Stepping inside his flat, his inner alarm began.

Too late.

The baseball bat tapped him smartly on the base of his skull and two thoughts burned as the carpet rushed to meet him.

a) Not this shit again

b) The carpet sure is worn

When he came to, many pains jostled for supremacy – his head… the rope round his neck… the ache in his lower back…

The Alien said, 'I wouldn't move if I were you. See, what I've done is tie a rope round your neck and connected it to yer feet. You move either, you slow strangle. But, don't sweat it – you'll catch on quick.'

Brant tried to move and the strangle hold tightened. He went: 'Urgh…uh…'

And Fenton said, 'Exactly! I think you've got it.'

Brant's pants and Y-fronts were around his ankles and he felt a baseball bat lightly tap his bum. For a horrific moment, he envisaged rape of an American variety.

Fen said, 'I hear you're a hard ass. Time to change that. For the next few weeks when you try to sit, remember: keep yer bloody nose outta people's business.'

A whistle began to scream from the kitchen and Fen said, 'I put the kettle on. Handy, those whistle tops, eh? No boiling over. Excuse me a mo!'

Brant was awash in cold sweat. Rivers of it coursing down his torso. Fear was roaring in his head.

Then, 'Okey-dokey… here we go. I'll pour…'

And white hot pain electrified Brant's brain.

✝

Fiona Roberts was stalled in traffic. Cars were blocked all

the way down to the Elephant. Her husband had many proclamations, most of a police bent. Among them was, 'If you're caught in traffic, keep the windows shut.'

Yeah, yeah.

She could hear a blast of rap from a nearby car and glanced over. A man with dreadlocks was giving large to a mobile. How he could hear anything above the music would be nothing short of miraculous. He caught her eye and gave a huge dazzling gold capped smile. Not too sure about her response, she looked away. Didn't do to encourage the game. A woman's head appeared at her elbow and a distinctly Irish accent whined, 'Gis the price of a cuppa tea, missus, and I'll say a prayer for ya.'

Fiona had never mastered the art of street encounters. As a cop's wife she'd learned zero except the response of confusion.

Like now. She muttered, 'I've no change.'

And the woman spat in her face.

The shock was enormous. As the spittle slid down her cheek, a symphony of horns began and shouts: 'Eh, get a bloody move on!' 'Shift yer knickers darlin'!'

She did. As the Americans say – 'Who ya gonna call?'

Her husband would crow, 'What did I say? ... Didn't I tell you about windows, eh? Didn't I say?'

The Ford Anglia 205E saloon is a classic. You gaze at it, you can almost believe the fifties and sixties had some worth. See your reflection in the chromed wing mirrors, you can almost imagine you have a quiff stuck in Brylcreem heaven with sleek brushed sideburns. The wheels are a collectors wet dream – rubber tyres with separate chrome hubcaps. Note that word 'separate'. The difference twixt class and mediocrity. Ask Honda as you whisper British Leyland. Throw in Harley Davidson and you've got one pissed off Jap. Roberts called his Anglia 'Betsy'. In the fifties, it was easier to name the car than the child. Roberts was financially strapped. A mortgage in Dulwich, a daughter in

21

boarding school. And he was hurting big time. Now that he'd been diagnosed with skin cancer, he'd flung the lot – caution, care, budget – to the cancerous wind.

The car was a bust. It didn't overstretch his finances so much as shout BLITZKRIEG.

He wasn't sorry, not one little bit. He loved – nay, *adored* – it. Kept it in a lock-up at Victoria. The garage belonged to a mate of Brant's and he was glad to oblige the police. Well glad-ish. Come a pale rider. In the nineties in London. Come joy riders. Bringing anything but joy.

Patience isn't high on their list of characteristics. They opened the lock-up no problem, but couldn't get the Anglia to start. So… so they burned it where it was. The fire took out three other garages.

When Roberts arrived, the blaze had been brought under control, but too late to save anything. The fire chief asked, 'That your motor in there?'

'Was.'

'You'll be insured?'

Roberts gave him the look. 'I'm a cop – what do *you* think?'

'Uh-oh.'

'Yeah.'

They watched the flames for a bit and then the chief said, 'There's a cup o' tea going… fancy one?'

'I don't think tea will do it.'

'You could be right. Me, I take comfort where I find it.'

'Gee, how philosophical… maybe I should be glad the fire gives heat to the neighbours.'

'See – you're sounding better already.'

Before Roberts could respond to this gem, his bleeper went and the Chief said, 'Could be a long night.'

'It's been a long fuckin' life, I tell you.'

But the Chief already knew that.

As Roberts sighed and turned away he ran a turn through his favourite noir movies. Always from the forties

22

and fifties. What surfaced was Barbara Stanwyck to Keith Andes in *Clash By Night*:

'What do you want, Joe, my life history? Here it is in four words:

BIG IDEAS, SMALL RESULTS.'

Yeah, the story of it all.

✝

Brant had passed out from shock. Now, as he came to, he curled up in anticipation of horrendous pain.

Curled up?

He thought – *What?* – and rolled easily onto his side. No pain. No rope.

Trembling, he moved his hand to his ass… wet and cold.

Cold water.

He'd been suckered with the oldest psych trick in the book.

Rage and relief fought for supremacy as he got shakily to his feet. Stumbled to the cupboard and got a bottle of Black Bushmills. He'd been keeping it for a four star moment like getting the knickers off Fiona Roberts. Twisted the top savagely, let the cap fall and chugged direct. Did this bastard burn… oh yeah!

He leaned against the cupboard and waited for the four stars to kick in. They did. Fast. And he muttered, 'Jaysus.'

After a few more slugs, he moved to the armchair and with a steady hand, lit a Weight. He knew who his assailant was. The so called 'Alien', the legendary fuck. Only one person would have the balls to set him loose. With Fenton it was just a job, but to the one calling the shots, it was personal. Brant began to savour how he'd boil the two of 'em together. Not with bloody cold water either.

Leigh Richards was a snitch. What's more, he was Falls' snitch, passed on by Brant who said, 'The most vital tool for police work is a grass. One of their own who'll turn for revenge, spite or money. But mainly money. Fear, too, that helps. I'm giving you this piece of garbage, 'cos I can no longer stomach 'im.'

After meeting Leigh, Falls could understand why. years ago, Edward Woodward made his name playing a character called Callan. He had a sidekick named Lonely. Leigh was the Lonely of the turn of the century. No specific reason that made him distasteful. Everything about him was ordinary. So much so that he looked like a photo-kit. Everybody and nobody. If there's such a thing as auras, then his spelt 'repellent'.

He said to Falls, 'This is a new departure for me.'

'What?'

'Working with a woman.'

Falls had a constant urge to lash out at him. Ordinarily, she was no testier than yourr average Northern Line commuter, but once in Leigh's presence, she felt murderous. She said slowly, 'Listen, shithead, we're *not* working together. We never have, never will – am I getting this across?'

He had his hair cut in a French crop. This is a crew-cut with notions. His eyes never met yours, and yet, he never ceased watching you. That's what Falls felt – she felt *watched*.

24

He put up his hands in mock surrender, said, 'Whoa, little lady! No offence meant.

I like niggers, anyone will tell you Leigh Richards isn't a bigot. Go on, ask anybody... you'll see. Live and let live is my motto.'

If Falls had sought Roberts' advice, he'd have said, 'Never trust a grass.' He knew from bitter experience. More, he could have recounted the lines from *The Thin Man*:

> *I don't like crooks.*
> *And If I did like them, I wouldn't like crooks who are*
> *stool pigeons.*
> *And if I did like crooks who are stool pigeons, I still*
> *wouldn't like you.'*

Roberts would have liked to rattle off the lines anyway because he liked to. Plus, he'd love to have been Nora Charles' husband. But she didn't ask and the lines stayed on celluloid – unwatched and unused.

Instead, Falls counted to ten and then she smacked Leigh in the mouth. His feelings, not to mention his mouth, were hurt.

He said, 'My feelings are hurt,' and he figured it was time to rein Falls in. Let her see a little of his knowledge, know who she was dealing with. He said, 'I know you. I know yer Dad died recent, and more, you couldn't cough up the readies to plant him.' He had her attention and continued, 'My old Dad snuffed it too. See this belt?'

In spite of herself, she looked. It appeared to be a boy scout one, right down to the odd buckle.

'When I went to the morgue, the guy said: "It's all he left, shall I sling it?" *Oi!* I said, *that's my estate!*'

Falls didn't smile, but Leigh could go with that. He'd smacked her right back and never even had to raise his hand or his voice.

She asked, 'There's a moral in there?'

'Like the great man said – "Be prepared!" '

'Who?'

'Baden Powell, founder of the scouts.'

Falls gave a harsh chuckle, said, 'They weren't real popular in Brixton.'

'Oh...'

'But let me give *you* a little story.'

Leigh didn't care for the light in her eye. He'd heard blacks got funny when they mentioned Brixton. Shit – when *anybody* mentioned it. He said: 'There's no need.'

'I insist. The cat asked: "Do you purr?" "No," said the ugly duckling. "Then you'll have to go." ' She let Leigh digest this then, 'So, you're a snitch... then *snitch*.'

'I'll need paying.'

'After.'

'It's good information.'

'Mr Brant was anxious to locate two Irish people, a man and a woman.'

'So?'

'He believes they can help with his... ahm... recent accident.'

'Do you know where they are?'

'I know where they went.'

'Yeah.'

'One of them was wearing a nice pair of Farahs as he boarded the plane – a plane for Amer-i-kay.'

In spite of herself, she uttered, 'Jesus.'

Leigh was excited, babbled on, 'According to my sources, a certain young copper was wearing said pants on the night of his demise.'

Falls grabbed both his wrists and, Brant-style, leant right into his face, said, 'Their names?'

'Josie... and Mick... that's all I know.'

She squeezed harder.

'Belton... OK! Mick Belton – you're hurting me!'

She let go, then reached in her purse and began to gather loose notes. He said in alarm, 'For Godsake, don't do it like that – palm it!'

She did and he squeezed her fingers during the move, said, 'I have a good feeling about us.'

'Yeah?' She sounded near warm.

Emboldened, he risked, 'You'll find me more than satisfactory in the… ahm…' And here he winked.

She whispered, 'And you ever talk to me like that, you'll find it in Brixton among the used condoms and other garbage.'

Then she was up and moving. He waited till she was a distance, then said, 'Yah lesbian!'

✝

The Alien was sitting in The Greyhound, in Bill's private corner. He was drinking a mineral water, slowly savouring the sparkle. Bill arrived with two minders. They branched off to man both ends of the bar. Fenton said, 'Impressive.'

Bill looked back at them. 'Yeah?'

'Oh definitely, real menace.'

Bill sat down and nodded to the barman. A bowl of soup was brought and two dry crackers. They were encased in that impossible to open plastic. Bill nodded at them, said, 'Get those, eh?'

'Why don't you call the muscle, give em a chance to flex.'

Bill smiled, 'You wouldn't be trying to wind me up would you Fen?'

'Naw, would I do that?'

Bill was quiet for a bit, then, 'You did the biz?'

'Course.'

'Didn't overdo it, did yah?'

'Naw, just put a frightener to him – he's mobile but dampened. You'll have no more strife.'

'I wouldn't want any of this coming back on me, Fen.'

'It's done, you've no worries. He's tamed – nowt for him now but nickel and dime till he gets his shitty pension. He's bottled out.'

27

Bill passed over a fat package. 'A little bonus, help you find yer feet in America… you'll be off soon.'

'Soon as shootin'.'

They both gave a professional laugh at this, not that either thought it as funny or even appropriate.

This is how the call came in.

'Hello, is that the police?'

The desk sergeant, weary after an all-nighter, answered, 'Yeah, can I help?' Not that he had a notion of so doing.

'I'm about to eat my breakfast.'

'How fascinating.'

'When I've finished, I'll wash up, and then I'm going to kill my old man.'

'Why's that then?'

'He molested me till I was twelve. Now I think he's going to start on my little brother...'

The sergeant was distracted by a drunk being manhandled by two young coppers. At the pitch of his lungs, he was singing: 'The sash my father wore...' No big deal in that, unless you noted the man was black. Thus perhaps giving credence to the expression 'a black protestant' or not.

When the sergeant got back to the call, he couldn't hear anyone on the line. Testily he repeated, 'Hello... yello?'

Then two shots rang clearly down the receiver and he knew, without thinking:

Shot gun – 12 gauge – double o cartridges

and muttered, *Jesus!'*

✝

A homeless person with a grubby T-shirt proclaimed, 'Jesus loves black and white but prefers Johnny Walker,' and touched Fiona Roberts on the arm. She jumped a foot off the ground thinking: 'They've even reached Dulwich'.

He said, 'Chill out, babe.' Even the displaced were going mid-Atlantic.

She ran. No dignity. No finesse. Out 'n' out legged it.

Inside her home she said aloud, 'I know! I'll never go out again – that'll do it.' And received a second jump when her daughter Sharon approached suddenly. 'Christ, Sharon, don't do that – sneaking up on a person.'

'Get real, Mom.'

Fiona thought: 'A nice cup o' tea, that will restore me,' and went to prepare it. She glanced in at the blaring TV. Regis and Kathy Lee were discussing manicures for dogs.

'Sharon... *Sharon*! Why is the telly so loud?... Why do you always need noise?'

The girl threw her eyes to heaven and sighed, 'You wouldn't understand.'

'What?... What's to understand? Tell me!'

Chewing on her bottom lip, the girl said, 'Cos yer *old*, Mum.'

Fiona scratched the tea and headed upstairs for a Valium – a whole shitpile of mother's little helpers... sorry, *old* mother's little helpers.

✝

When Charlie Kray, brother of the twins, tried to flog cocaine, three of his customers turned out to be undercover cops. A true sting. Over seventy, Charlie was found guilty, despite his own lawyer calling him a pathetic case. Who Charlie called was Bill. Like this.

'Bill?'

'Yeah.'

'It's Charlie.'

'Hi, son, I'm sorry about yer bit o' grief.'

'They set me up Bill.'

'I know, they put you right in the frame.'

'You know me, Bill – I 'ate drugs.'

'We wouldn't be 'aving this chat if it were otherwise.'

'Thanks, Bill. Reggie always said you were the bollocks.'

'Was there somefing, Charlie?'

'Is there owt you can do for us, mate? I go in, it's life… at my age.'

'Wish I could, son but it's solid. You're going down, but I can 'ave a word, make it cushy as possible.'

A pause. Defeat hanging full, then resignation.

'Yeah, righto Bill… Will you look out for my old girl?'

''Course, you don't 'ave to ask.'

'Maybe you'll get up my way, bring us in a bit o' cheer.'

'Course I will, soon as.'

But he never did. Bill wasn't a visitor and in this case he didn't even send the help.

That book was writ.

✝

When Roberts had proposed to Fiona, her family had raised huge objections. Roberts had told his own father of their view. His father, a man of few words, said, 'They're right.'

'What – you think I'm not good enough for her?'

'I wasn't thinking about you. As usual you've got it backwards.'

Roberts was pleased, then said, 'They've money.'

'Ah!... Well, perhaps you have class. Now it's possible we'll get money, whereas…'

He figured he'd call on Brant, maybe even talk about Fiona. But probably not. Brant's door was open and Roberts thought 'Uh-oh.'

Brant was sitting on the couch watching TV. Two bananas were coming down the stairs and singing.

31

Roberts said, 'What the hell are yah watching?'

'It's *Bananas in Pyjamas*, quite a catchy little tune.'

He turned round to stare at Roberts, who said, 'The door was open... I...'

'Hey, no sweat. Everybody else just walks in.'

'You had a visit?'

'Yeah, a villain with a message. Next, he'll have a chat show.'

Roberts moved in closer. 'Are you all right? Any damage?'

'Any damage. Hmm... he wanted to boil me bollocks and I speak not metaphorically here.'

'Jesus.'

'Yeah.'

'Can I get you anyfin'?'

Brant looked at the mug he was holding, said, 'It's tea.'

'Another?'

'Two sugs, Guv. It's them triangle jobs – and you know what? – they *do* taste better; like yer old Mum used to make.'

Roberts went to the kitchen and marvelled at the mess. Like squatters had staged a demo there. Brant shouted, 'Heat the cups.'

'Yeah, right.'

Once the tea was squared away, Roberts sat. 'You want to tell me what's going down?'

'Bill Preston.'

'Tell me you're winding me up. You haven't been sniffin' round in *his* biz... the order came from on high – hands off.'

'Let 'im run riot, that it?'

'They're building a case, it takes time.'

'Bollocks.'

'C'mon, Tom, the softly-softly approach will bring him in finally.'

'So meanwhile, we sit back and play with ourselves.'

'Shit! You started pushing him!'

'A bit.'

32

'And you got a visit. Who'd he send?'

'Fenton, last of the fuckin' Mohicans.'

'The Alien. You should be flattered – means you got their attention.'

'Yeah, that's what I am. Flattered.'

Roberts drained his tea and wondered if he'd have another. Thing was, you always regretted it.

Brant asked, 'Want 'nother brewski?'

'Love one.'

They did, and sure enough it had that stewed taste which British Rail have raised to an art. A sour tang of metal and over-indulgence.

Roberts said, 'You're going to leave it alone now.'

'Mm... phh!'

'C'mon Tom, walk away.'

Brant looked like he was seriously considering this as an option. They both knew otherwise, but as Roberts was the senior officer, he at least had to dance the charade.

Then Brant said, 'I was watching a documentary on the New York cops, it was on BBC2.'

'Yeah, any good?'

'When a drug dealer gets killed, the detectives say "Condition Corrected".'

Roberts smiled in spite of himself, stood and asked, 'Can we expect you at work any time, son?'

'Absolutely, soon as Regis and Kathy Lee finish.'

'Like them, do you?'

'Naw, it's just I can't distinguish one cunt from the other.'

Black as he's painted

When Falls had joined the force, she had near perfected a neutral accent. If the situation demanded, she could 'street' with ease, or float the Brixton patois… *and* twist her vowels to blend into south-east London like a good un.

Early on she'd fallen in love with a bloke from CID. He said he adored her blackness and appeared to have no hang-up of being seen with her. There were no derisory comments, as he had the 'cop face'. The one which says: 'Fuck with me and you'll fuckin rue the day'. Like that.

Finally, the time came when she had to know how he felt, and she asked, 'Jeff, how do you feel about me?'

Risky, risky, risky.

He said, 'Honey (sic), I really like you. And if I was going to settle down it would definitely be with you.'

Yeah. Sayonara sucker.

✝

After Roberts' departure, Brant remained in front of the TV, schemes of mayhem and destruction flicking fast through his head.

Dennis The Menace came on, an episode where the Menace was camping in the woods. A wild gorilla was loose and Dennis' father asked: 'Who'll warn the gorilla?'

Brant smiled. If he'd believed in omens he'd have called it a metaphor of fine timing.

34

Next up was Barney. Brant said aloud, 'I can't friggin' believe I'm watching an eight foot purple dinosaur with green polka dots... *singing*. And worse, *tap dancing*.'

Then, as if a cartoon light bulb went on over his head, Brant said, 'Wait a mo!' And knew how to proceed.

Over the past few years, he'd begun to acknowledge his Irish heritage. He'd begun to collect a motley pile of Irish paraphernalia, including ugly leprechauns, bent shillellighs, horrendous bodhrans and – yes, he still had it – a hurley.

Hurling is the Irish National game. A cross between hockey and murder. Now he pulled out the stick from beneath a mess of shamrocked T-shirts. Made from ash, it fits like a baseball bat. He gave it a trial swing and relished the *swoosh* as it sliced the air.

He shouted, 'Cul agus culini for Gaillimh!'

And added, 'Way to fuckin go, boyo!'

Exporting aliens

The Alien had one last look round his gaff, saw nothing he'd particularly miss. When you do hard time, it's nigh impossible to ever make a home. You get it all comfy, the screws come and move you or toss it or piss all over the floor.

Keep it simple. Keep it mobile.

He'd packed two pairs of black 501s – they were the old full-faded jobs he'd got in Kensington Market. In the days when people still spoke English in that part of London. Four Ben Sherman knock-offs and two white T-shirts. A pair of near new Bally loafers he'd found in Oxfam at Camden Lock. Did they fit like a glove? Put them on and they whispered, 'Is this heaven or what?' They were.

For travel, he'd a pair of non-iron khaki chinos and a blazer. Slide one of the white T-shirts inside, you were the Gap ideal.

Casual

Smart

Hip

He thought, 'Asshole!… Right.'

At the airport he bought a walkman and The Travelling Willburys. It reminded him of a mellowness he might have achieved. In Duty Free there was a promotion for Malibu. Caribbean rum with coconut.

Yeah.

Plus, he kinda liked the bottle. The sales assistant said, 'Boarding card?'

'We can do that.'

'Cash or charge?'

He smiled – this was not a south-east London girl – and produced a flush of crisp readies. 'Just made 'em.'

'I beg your pardon?'

'Hey, no need to beg, these are the jokes.'

She produced a garish T-shirt. 'It's free with purchases over twenty pounds.'

'Tell you what, hon, you wear it – help yah to loosen up, get the bug outta yer ass.'

The flight was delayed and Fenton said, 'Fuck.' Sat on a couch-type seat and unscrewed the Malibu.

He was about to sample when a voice said, 'I sincerely hope you're not thinking of drinking that.'

'What?'

He turned to see a yuppie guy of about thirty. Dressed in a spanking new Adidas tracksuit, he had a fifty quid haircut and cheap eyes. Said, 'One is not permitted to open Duty-Free before departure.'

Fenton put the cap back on the bottle, asked, 'If I drank it – just supposing I went ahead and took a swig – what exactly is it you'd do, then?'

The guy pursed his lips. Fenton had always thought it was only an expression, but no, the guy was doing just that. Then he gave a tight smile. 'Alas, one would feel it obligatory to inform someone of authority.'

'Ah!'

'If every chap flouted the rules, where would we be?'

Fenton didn't think it required an answer so he said nowt. Eventually the guy pushed off and Fen tracked him with his eyes. Sooner or later, the guy had to piss, right?

Right.

'You know the law isn't for people like us.'

'What is?'

'That's another thing I've been trying to figure out for years.'

(Lola Lane to Bette Davis in *Marked Woman*).

As Roberts walked towards The Greyhound, a holy-roller pressed a leaflet into his hand. He glanced at it, read:

'The God We Worship Carves His Name On Our Faces.'

He figured it might be true, especially as it was said that Brant had the devil's own face. The light in the pub was dark and it took a minute for his eyes to adjust. The barman asked, 'What can I do for you, John?'

'Eh?'

'A drink. You want one or not?'

'Is Bill here?'

'Who's asking?'

Roberts leant over the counter, not sure he'd heard it right, then decided to go for it. 'Tell him it's the *Old* Bill.'

He wasn't sure but he thought he heard a malicious laugh. Bill was in his usual place and if not master of all he saw, he certainly had its attention. A novel lay opened in front of him, one of the Charlie Resnick series by John Harvey. Roberts glanced at the title – *Rough Treatment*.

Bill said, 'My kind of copper.'

Roberts didn't think he meant him. 'Mind if I join you?'

'No, I don't mind. Get you somefin'?'

'Nice toasted sarnie I reckon, I missed breakfast.'

'They do a good un here, cheese, tomato… shoot the works.'

'Course.'

That done, they sat in silence a bit. Their relationship went back a long way, almost the old code. When villains kept villainy internal and cops kept some other agenda. More a show of respect than any actual feel for it.

The sandwich came and Roberts got right to it. As he finished the first half Bill said, 'Jeez, you did miss brekkie.'

'Yeah, we had a son kill his old man – phoned it in himself.'

'Funny old world, eh?'

Roberts pushed the plate away. 'How's Chelsea?'

Bill had a daughter with Down's syndrome. Now seven years old, she was the true joy of his life, his one vulnerability. 'She's doing good, full o' verbals.'

Thus the pleasantries, time for biz.

Roberts tried to inject hard into his voice, not too much, but there. 'My sergeant got a call.'

'Yeah?'

'That's Detective Sergeant Brant.'

'A man of reckless inclination.'

'He'll want to see the messenger.'

'Ah!'

'Keep up appearances on every side, can't have some laddie shoutin' the odds in his local.'

'No fear.'

'Why's that then?'

'Took a trip, to America.'

'Sudden.'

'A mad desire to see his missus.'

'I wouldn't want to have this chat again... *Bill*.' It sounded like what it was – a threat.

Bill said tightly, 'I'm a bit confused over yer concern for the said Sergeant.'

'We've got mileage.'

Bill considered then went for the cut. 'You're a big hearted bloke, Mr Roberts.'

'Eh?'

'Well, if one of my lads was putting it to me missus, I'd be more than a tad miffed.'

Roberts was taken aback, near lost it, but rallied. 'Low shot, Bill, I'd have figured you for a more mature angle.'

Bill didn't answer. Roberts stood, put some money on the table and walked away.

At the door he heard, 'Hey Old Bill, Brant likes maturity. You ask down the nick – he likes 'em downright middle aged.'

Falls had the golden oldies show playing. Playing loud.

Jennifer Rush with 'The Power of Love'.

A sucker song.

As she belted out the lyrics, Falls threw in the obligatory *Oh*s… *Uh*s… and hot *Ah*s… Being black helped cos she felt the music.

Reluctantly, she turned the radio off. Being hot at nine in the morning was wasted heat. She put on a light khaki T-shirt, loose and blousey. Then white needle cords, very washed, very faded. A dream to wear, like skin that didn't cling. At the dentist, she'd flicked through a copy of *Ebony* and read that needle cord was coming back.

Where had they been?

She thought: 'Not this pair. One more wash and it's disintegration city.'

Checking the date of the magazine, it was February '88.

Oh.

Falls felt lucky wearing these pants. Plus, she felt hip, not big time or to the point of wearing sunglasses on her hair, but a player. She was wearing a black pair of Keds. They made her feet look tiny and she wished she could wear them in bed. And might yet do so.

Opening her front door, she felt downright optimistic.

Always a bad start.

A skinhead was spraying her wall, it read:

NAZZI RULES? OK.

He was a young fifteen with badly applied tattoos, the usual Doc Martens and black combat trousers. The spraying stopped and his eyes said *run*. But even a junior skin couldn't be seen to run from a woman, especially a black one. He fingered the aerosol nervously and pushed out his chest.

40

Falls asked, 'Who's Nazzi?'

'What, doncha know?'

'No.'

'Like Gestapo and shit, ya know.'

'Oh, *Nazi*.'

'Yeah.'

'Then you've spelt it wrong.'

'Ya what?'

'One "z".'

He looked at his handiwork, unsure as to what she meant. But hey, if confused, attack. The first rule of the urban warrior. 'So what? Wogs can't read.'

Falls did the very worst thing. She laughed. The boy didn't know which was next:

fight

or

flight.

Fighting required the pack and flight was... available. Just.

To add to his turmoil, she smiled, said, 'Nice chattin' to you but I've got to go.'

'You gonna report me?'

'Naw.'

'Don't you mind, then, me doin' yer wall?'

'Oh I mind, I just don't mind a whole lot.'

As she headed off, he shouted, 'Don't suppose ya got the price of a cup o' tea?'

And stunned him by giving over some coins. Before he could think he said, 'Jeez, thanks a lot missus.'

She said, 'Why not skip the tea and buy a dictionary?'

Part of him wanted to roar, 'I can spell cunt.'

But he couldn't bring himself to. As he watched her go, he had his first mature observation.

'She's got some moves.'

Ticket to ride

As Fenton's flight levelled out over Heathrow, he unbuckled the seat belt and stretched his legs. A flight for New York was further delayed due to a missing passenger. Later, he'd be found in the toilet booth, both halves of his torn ticket protruding from his arse.

The passenger next to Fenton reached out his hand, said, 'Hi guy, I'm Skip.'

Fenton said, 'You're kidding!' and thought, 'Lemme see... like, nine hours beside this wanker... Jesus!'

Unperturbed, the man said, 'I'm in software out of Illinois. How do you guys stick that damp climate?'

Fenton straightened up, looked the man in both eyes, said, 'Skip it.'

Barney is a dinosaur from our imagination

Bill remembered his old man. The last time he saw him he'd gone to meet him in a pub at Stockwell. The old man was a cap in hand merchant. Sitting at the counter, the cap on the stool beside him, he was nursing a small whiskey.

Bill was on his uppers, flush with the takings from a series of post offices. He said, 'Dad, what can I get you?'

'I'm drinking on the clock, son.'

Bill knew about 'drinking on the slate'. You didn't grow up in Peckham without learning that and fast. 'What?'

'I've enough for three drinks – if I make each last an hour, I'll be up to lunchtime.'

'Jeez, here...' Bill laid a wedge on the bar. The old man never even glanced at it said, 'Give it to yer Mother.'

'Fuck her.'

And his father turned, eyes flashing, hand raised. Not clenched, but definitely ready. 'Don't you curse her. Mum, she had it hard.'

'She legged it, didn't she?'

His father sighed. 'Go away son, I can't watch right with you here.'

Yeah.

When his old man was being planted, Bill was standing over the grave and threw a wrist watch in after the box.

43

'Clock that.'

Bill was musing on this as his daughter played along the Embankment. Every Thursday they came there, he'd sit on the bench and she'd stand watching the cruise boats. Nothing gave her as much joy.

When he'd asked why, she said, 'Cos boats make people happy.'

Argue that.

Her having Down's syndrome meant she had an extra chromosome. Or, as he now believed, *normal* people had one missing. Whatever. She meant so much to him it hurt. He'd always said: 'Hope I never have a daughter', because he knew she'd make him vulnerable and that was the one thing he couldn't be. Now here she was, and left him with an Achilles heel. But it was worth it for all his worry – she lit up his life like nothing ever had. And lit it more every passing day. If having a child changes you, having a child with Down's syndrome changes you entirely.

Thus preoccupied he'd taken his eyes off his daughter. Then snapped back and turned to see her.

No Chelsea.

Heart pounding, he jumped to his feet, heard, 'Hey asshole, this way.'

Turned to see Brant holding the girl in his arms, dangerously close to the high bar of the Embankment.

Brant held out one hand, a furry toy hanging loose. 'I got Barney for her, seems to work.' Bill took a step forward and Brant cautioned, 'I wouldn't do that boyo; you don't want to startle a dinosaur – they're unpredictable.'

Bill tried to keep calm. Brant was one crazy fucker, built a rep on it. Looked round, not a sign of his bloody minders, asked, 'What do you want, Brant?'

'Fenton.'

'He's gone to San Francisco.'

'Bit of a holiday, is it?'

'He's tracking his ex-wife.'

Brant swung the little girl up above the railing, the dinosaur held against her. 'See Bill, I want you to know how easy it is to touch you. You stay the hell away from me, everything's hunky-dory.'

'I hear what you're saying.'

'I wonder, Bill. I wonder if you do. Perhaps a demonstration...' And he let go. The purple dinosaur tumbled down, its small head bounced off the bottom bar, then it rolled on the concrete before it slid into the water.

It sank quickly.

'Jesus,' breathed Bill.

Brant let the girl down and nodded towards the water. 'Just wasn't getting the ratings anymore.'

The girl ran to her father and wrapped her arms round him, cried, 'Dad, Barney's gone.'

'It's OK, sweetheart, it's OK...'

Brant started to move away, not hurried but measured. 'See how it goes, Bill? Dinos are past their sell-by date.'

On break the 12th lament

Falls read the words aloud.

'Her evocation then of all that mystery allures'

She hadn't one clue what it meant but never-no-mind – she adored it. In the canteen with her friend Rosie, she asked, 'Do you know what it means?'

'Not a clue.'

'Me neither.'

'But it sounds kinda, I dunno… sexy.'

Falls looked down then said, 'I always wished I'd have them boobs that jiggle, you know – if you're running, they'd hop up 'n' down.'

Rosie, who was more than endowed, shook her head. 'No you don't… believe me.'

'Men prefer big boobs.'

'Men are pigs.'

And they laughed. Falls got serious and said, 'Rosie, I'm worried.'

'What, that men are pigs?'

'No…I've been sick three mornings…'

Rosie shrieked, 'Oh God, are you…?'

Falls shushed her quick, said, 'Jeez, keep it down!'

'You're telling the wrong person, me girl.'

And they got the serial giggles. Lots of the cops glared. If there was laughing to be done, the men would do it.

Rosie lowered her voice. 'You've got to find out.'

'Oh God, I can't!'

'Get one of those do-it-yourself tests from Boots.'

Further speculation was halted as the duty sergeant put his head round the door and shouted: 'We've got a would-be rapist shot!' A cheer went up. 'Oi, that's enough of that. I need two WPCs… c'mon, snap to it.'

As they headed out Falls said, 'Leastways if I am I'll get decent boobs.'

Rosie laughed. 'You'll be jiggling more than them!'

✝

The shooting had taken place off Camberwell Green. A man had attacked a woman in her kitchen, but she broke away and somehow managed to shoot him.

The flat was packed with cops. Falls was directed to the woman. She was sitting on a kitchen chair, her face white with shock. A loud moaning could be heard from the sitting room. Falls closed the door.

The woman asked, 'Is that him?'

'I think so.'

'I thought I'd killed him.'

Falls patted her shoulder, asked 'Like a cup o' tea love?'

'I'm sick of tea.'

'Do you want to talk about what happened?'

'I was washing up and next thing I was grabbed… but I've been taking classes… in self defence. So I stomped on his instep and bit his arm.'

'Good girl.'

The woman was animated, into it. 'He let go and I hit him with the saucepan – here.' She indicated her chin. 'And I heard a crack. He started roaring and I walked out to the sitting room. Got my Dad's gun and then… I shot him. I missed a few times, I think.'

When everything was being wrapped, the woman touched Falls' hand. 'What will they do to me?'

'Well, I think you'll get off, but I believe you should get a medal.'

47

The man had been shot once in the upper leg. Once on the stretcher, Falls managed to get near him. He said, 'The bitch tried to kill me… I'll sue…'

Falls leant over, asked in a soft voice, 'Does it hurt?'

He gave a macho smile. 'No, it's not so bad.'

Falls shot out her hand, pounded once on the wound. 'Any better?'

Lies are the oil of social machinery (Proust)

When Brant heard of Falls' treatment of the rapist, he was well delighted, thought: 'Yer coming along, lassie.'

He'd been to see the Super and been granted a period of leave. Twixt sickdays and holidays, he'd a block of time owing.

The Super, keen to be rid of him, suggested, 'Might be time to consider getting out.'

Brant gave a police manual smile, a mix of servility, spite and animal cunning, and said, 'We'd miss you, sir.'

He headed to the canteen and met Roberts en route, said, 'Lemme get you a tea, Guv.'

'And you'll pay for it.'

'Course.'

'It would be a first.'

In the canteen, Brant got two Club Milks and two sweetened coffees, then said to the cashier, 'Bung it on the Chief Inspector's tab.'

'We don't 'ave one.'

'Time to start, boyo.'

Roberts couldn't get Bill's accusation out of his head, that Brant had been with his wife. He said, 'I went to see Bill.'

'Oh yeah.'

'Tried to wind me up.'

'How's that?'

'Said you'd been jumping my missus.'

Brant's heart jumped, but said smoothly, 'Jeez, would I be so stupid?… I mean… apart from everything, I'd like to think we were mates.'

They both tasted the lie, let it roll around a bit and decided it would suffice. Not great or even satisfactory but almost sufficient… it would do.

Brant ate his Club Milk. First he nibbled the chocolate round the edge, then chomped the biscuit loudly. Roberts had a horrible picture of him nibbling his wife.

Brant gestured to the second biscuit. 'Going to have it, Guv?'

Roberts wasn't, but no way could he stomach Brant eating it. 'I'll get to it later.' He slipped it into his pocket. Days later, after his first radiation treatment, he'd find it congealed in his hankie, latched to his keys like a tumour.

Brant said, 'I watched *The Missouri Breaks* last night.'

'Yeah?'

'I love that boyo, Harry Dean Stanton. He's one of a battered outlaw gang led by Jack Nicholson. He tells a great yarn.' Brant stopped and Roberts didn't say anything. A tad testy, Brant asked, 'You want to hear this story or not?'

'Oh… yeah, of course.'

'He says when he was a kid, he had a favourite dog. One day his father came home and found the dog with its nose in the butter, so he shot it. Later on, a guy says to Harry Dean: "You don't like people much" – and Harry says – "Not since the dog put his nose in the butter".'

Roberts wasn't sure how to respond and finally said lamely, 'Must see that.'

Brant was agitated, asked, 'Don't you get it?'

'Course I do.' But he didn't. Worse, they both understood that. A moment comes, a friendship can move up a notch or is lost.

The moment was lost irretrievably.

They have to get you in the end
Otherwise there'd be no end to the pointlessness

(Derek Raymond)

'Yo, fool…'

This was Fenton's introduction. He'd arrived at SFIP (San Francisco International Passport) and breezed through Immigration. Manners and a British accent being a passport all their own. The official had even said, 'Y'all have a good day now.'

He was having one… sort of… ish.

Until:

Waiting on his luggage a black guy had shouted the above. Fenton turned, saw the guy dressed in an impoverished Mr T style. Lots of gold bracelets, medallions, but of a distinctly tin quality.

Fenton asked, 'Are you talking to me fella?'

'Whatcha think? Y'o be a fool, then I talking to you, mother fuckah.'

If this had been the Oval, he'd probably have drop-kicked him for exercise. Instead he smiled and got, 'Wha'cha smiling fo' bro'? Yo be laughin at de brother?'

Fenton got his case, turned and said, 'Get me a taxi – sorry – a *cab*… OK?'

This stopped the guy dead. While he was figuring it, Fenton breezed past him. 'Jeez, before Tuesday, OK?'

On the other side of the United States, the band-aiders were finding that the BIG APPLE was not exactly the good apple.

Still wearing the Farah pants, the guy said to the woman, 'This place's a hole.'

'Was your idea to come.'

'Was not.'

'Was too.'

They seethed a while, then the woman said, 'Let's mug some fuck and go to California.'

He liked that, said, 'I like that. Yeah. Let's kick the bejaysus outta a Yank.'

'Yeah… and tell 'em to have a nice day.'

In my last darkness there
might not be the same need
of understanding anything
so far away as the world
any more.

(Robin Cook)

Roberts was an hour early for his radiation treatment.
Got to wait three more. Eventually his time. He said,
'Does it hurt?'

'Huh?'

The radiation, you know, during the… ahm… process…'

The technician, with a distracted air seemed to have
trouble concentrating. Roberts wanted to grab him, roar,
'For fucksake, focus!'

The guy wasn't actually wearing a walkman but he
might as well have been. Worse, he was humming… and
humming 'Vienna'. Not an easy task, but definitely irritating. He said, 'Imagine yer on a sun bed, topping up for yer
hols.'

Roberts felt this was in particular bad taste in light of his
complaint, but said nothing. It wouldn't do to antagonise
the hand on the machine.

It didn't take long. Roberts asked, 'Is that it?'

'Yup, yer toast.'

Roberts felt a rush of elation and wanted to hug the fuck,
but the guy was already humming a new tune. Sounded like
the Eagles' 'Lying Eyes', or was it 'Dancing Queen'?

Roberts said, 'I'll be off then.'

'Whatever.'

Roberts had been a cop so long, it was difficult to surprise him. But every now and again…

Outside, three winos were sitting against the wall. All were shoeless. A pair of black shoes sat in front of them. Mid-way polished, they stood in near dignity and in reasonable condition A hand-written sign said,

FOR SALE
Only one owner.
£5 or nearest offer.
Full MOT.

He smiled from way down. One of the winos copped him, said, 'Size 9, Guv?'

Reaching in his pocket, he encountered a melted Club Milk latched to his keys. Finally, he located some coins and handed them over. One of them said

'God bless you, Guv.'

Further along, a young woman pushed a collection box in his face, demanded, 'Buy a flag.'

'What's it for?'

'Racquet Club in Hampstead.'

'Well that's badly needed – another sports club in bleeding Hampstead.' He gave her the remains of the Club Milk.

At the Oval, to complete his trilogy of street encounters, he bought a copy of *The Big Issue*. The vendor said, 'Fair cop,' and Roberts wondered what it was that proclaimed him to the world as a copper. He wasn't sure he wanted to know.

Castro

The Castro in San Francisco has been called 'The gayest place on earth'.

Fenton was headed there. He knew it would be the centre for activists. Now that Stell, his ex-wife was with a teacher, she'd be politically active. A dormant radical, she'd blossom in the Castro.

He had the cab cruise through Market and Castro Streets. It reminded him of Camden Lock on a pink Saturday. Same sex couples strolling openly. The cabbie turned and drove along Church, 22nd, and Duboce.

'You figger on stayin' here, buddy?'

'Naw, I just wanted to see it.'

The driver checked him in the mirror, ventured, 'You gotta get down here in the evenings, catch the action then.' He let the question hang in the air – *Are you gay or what?*

Fenton didn't help and kept staring out the window. He half believed he'd see her on the street. Just like that! After all the years, all the hate, there she'd be. She wasn't. He got a mental grip and said, 'I've seen enough, take me to the El Drisco.'

'Say again?'

Fenton consulted his guide book, nodded and said, 'It's 2901 Pacific Avenue.'

'Gonna cost you, buddy.'

'Did I ask you for a financial opinion?'

The cabbie took another look and decided to let it slide.

'You're the man.'

'So they tell me.'

✝

The constables had organised a knees-up in The Greyhound for Brant's departure. They had the back room and the booze was flowing. Word had got to Bill about the function so he'd relinquished his usual place. He could wait.

Sometimes, it was what he did best.

Brant was top of his shit list yet again but he wanted something major. For now, he simmered.

Brant was mid-pint and mid-story. 'So, the guy had tried to pay the hooker with a stolen credit card. The pimp was kicking the bejaysus outta him and the guy's shouting: "Be fair mate!" '

Falls arrived, and went, 'Uh-oh, boys at play.'

Someone shoved a drink at her and a plate of cocktail sausages. That made her smile. Brant swaggered over, said, 'Memories, eh?'

She put the plate aside, thinking: 'They never rose to that length!' She said, 'I have a going away pressie for you.'

'I'll be back.'

'Of that I've no doubt.' She handed him an envelope. He shook it loose and found two photos. They were from those platform machines, the quick-snap jobs that ensure you look like Myra Hindley, regardless of sex. A sheet of paper was clipped to them.

'What's this?'

'It's the Band-Aiders, the two who stabbed you and maybe killed Tone. They've gone to America.'

'Nice one, Falls.'

Her bleeper went and she headed for the phone. On her return, Brant hadn't moved. She said, 'A fire in East Lane… and deliberate. You think it's our man?'

56

'Want me to come visit him with you again?'

'No Sarge, no need, you enjoy the party.'

She was wrong. There was ample need for Brant. Then and later. Especially later.

Roberts arrived late at the party. Brant, his face flushed from drink, said, 'We started without you.'

'Oh really?' And got two mangled sausages handed to him, plus a pint of flat Guinness. 'What a feast.'

'Ah, we didn't forget you Guv.'

Roberts let the sausages slip to the floor and said, 'You're off, then.'

'Yeah, I'm going via Ireland from Shannon, so I'm going up to Galway for a night. I've a distant cousin there name of Paddy Joyce.'

'Related to James, no doubt.'

Brant gave him a puzzled, befuddled look. 'No... related to me, I said.'

'Whatever. Here.'

And he too produced a slip of paper. Brant said, 'Jaysus, I've more notes than Rymans.'

'It's the number of an American cop. He was over here on a course a few years back. He might be useful.'

Brant was slipping from the booze high to a mid-plateau of surliness, just before sentimentality. 'Don't need no Yank, I've got me hurley.'

'Yer what?'

But a sing-song had started and Brant was moving away. Roberts felt a bone exhaustion begin and a raging thirst. As he made his exit, he could hear Brant, loudest of all with 'If you ever go across the sea to Ireland...'

✟

When Falls had applied to the police force, she'd had to wait six months. *The Bill* was hot then and they were flooded

57

with applications, even wannabe actresses who believed they'd be doing the method.

During that period, Falls worked in a department store. She was assigned to Customer Services and dealt with returned items. It was the ideal training for police work. Here came the scum of the earth, the true dissatisfied. The more respectable the customer, the more brazen the lie. They'd bring back blouses, the collar soiled, lipstick on the front, creased to infinity, and claim: Never Worn!

Receipts years out of date and frequently from other stores were produced in apparent innocence. A week on this front made her a cynic for life. And of course she got the full dose of bigotry. Like, 'I demand to see someone in authority. Someone white in authority.'

The up-side was Falls could spot a liar at close range. The downside, apart from insults, aggression and bile, was that she could never again return goods. No matter how press-ing the urge. The girls thus employed went two ways – became immune or became traffic wardens, which amounted to the same thing.

Falls broke the cardinal rule of visiting a suspect alone. She hoped she might wrap the deal in one evening.

She was wrong.

Calling on the suspected arsonist, she was pumped with adrenalin.

For nowt.

A woman answered the door. In her early twenties, she was barefoot in shorts and Spice Girls top, said, 'Yeah?'

'I'm WPC Falls and...'

The woman put up a hand, signalling *don't bother* and said, 'He's not here. Dunno when he'll be back. I've no idea where he is.' Said this to the tune of 'Mary had a little lamb'. Said it with world weariness. Like, how many times have I to repeat this shit?

Her eyes were deep blue and deeper stoned. If she'd

58

recently touched planet earth, she hadn't much liked it. Her expression moved to:

You know I'm lying.

I know you know I'm lying.

So whatcha gonna do about it, bitch?

Not a whole lot, save: 'And you are…?'

'Oprah Winfrey, can't you tell?'

Falls shook her head. 'Gee, that's an amusing line. Well Oprah, I'll be back. Often. See how that helps the ratings.'

The woman slammed the door and Falls figured that whatever else the woman was, intimidated wasn't part of it.

She knew if Brant had been with her, the result would be completely different. Not legal, maybe not even satisfactory, but definitely radical. And thinking of results, she had an appointment in the morning with her GP. Find out if she was pregnant / with child / knocked up / in the family way. As the various expressions ran through her head, she felt both exhilarated and terrified.

Two feelings not unknown to the man across the street. Standing in a doorway, he watched her walk away. When he usually got these feelings, it was immediately after he'd tossed the match to his work.

Excitement gripped him now as he wondered how the black woman would burn.

Americana

The Alien was well pleased with his hotel. The El Drisco, on Pacific Avenue is one of those open secrets. Owned and operated by the same family since the twenties; Eisenhower and Truman had made visits. It sure looked presidential – deep pile carpets, green leather banquettes, crystal chandeliers... Like that. For a moderate arm and leg it's worth getting the hillside view.

The receptionist had told Fenton the guest rooms were much more reasonable; but Fenton said, 'I'm only doing it one time. Best to do it right, eh?'

The receptionist agreed that this was indeed a fine method of reasoning. Back in London a similar response would have been dangerously close to taking the piss. Here it was the American way.

In his room, Fenton stretched out on the bed, thought: *One or two days to find Stell and kill her... and maybe grab a few days rest and recreation in Tijuana...* 'Yeah,' he said aloud. 'I like the sound of that R & R...'

Fenton liked San Francisco. He was beginning to like it a whole lot. That it's very much a walking city didn't hurt, didn't hurt at all. Twixt cabs, trolley and foot, he got to Fisherman's Wharf.

The cabbie had said, 'Yo buddy, a real native is a guy who's never had eats at The Wharf. You hear what I'm saying?'

The Alien hadn't quite got into the sheer *in yer face* dialogue, as if they'd known you always. He answered, 'Course I hear you... I'm not deaf.'

The cabbie took a look back. 'English, right?'

'How perceptive.'

Unfazed. 'I love the way you guys talk, like Masterpiece Theatre. Everyone talks like that in England, am I right?'

Jesus! 'Yeah... except for the taxis – they shut it.'

'That's like the cabs, right?'

Getting out at the Wharf, Fenton paid, and sure enough the cabbie said, 'You have a good day.'

'Whatever.'

Fenton went straight for a bar. He was wearing thin on American goodwill. The barman welcomed him effusively.

Fenton said, 'Give us a beer, OK?'

'Domestic or imported?'

'Fuck.'

Fenton was the other side of three bottles of Bud. Not outta it or even floating, but feeling them, a nice buzz building. He figured he'd do three more then go buy the baseball bat.

An exaggerated English accent cut through: 'I say old chap, might I trouble you for a light?'

Fenton turned. On the stool beside him was a guy in his bad sixties. Liver spots on his hands and brown shorts, top to accessorise. He had eyes that Fenton could only think of as stupid, i.e. eager, friendly and open.

Fenton shrugged. He was definitely feeling those beers. 'I don't smoke.'

'Actually, neither do I – I heard you order your drink and thought I'd give my skills a try. Was I convincing?'

'As what?'

'Oh yes, the English humour! I have all of Monty Python, would you like to see my Ministry of Funny Walks?'

'You're serious... Jesus!'

'You might have caught me on Seinfeld, I was the English cab driver.'

Fenton was suddenly tired, the beers wilted, the show winding down. He asked, 'You're an actor… act scared.'

'Scared?'

'Yeah, as if I'm going to put this bottle up yer arse.'

The man looked full into Fenton's face and got a hearty slap on the shoulder, with, 'Hey, that's not bad, you look like you could shit yerself…I'm impressed.'

After Fenton left the bar, he was entranced by the traffic lights, blinking:

WALK

DON'T WALK

No frills, yer straight command. He kinda appreciated it – reminded him of prison.

A black guy in a combat jacket was handing out pamphlets, shouting, 'Yo', homies, see what de fat cats be doin' wit' yo' tax dollars!'

Fen took the booklet. 'Ain't my tax dollars, mate.'

'Say what, homey?'

He was about to sling it as the guy shouted, 'Yo' all gots de right to know they be killin' folk.'

Fenton looked at the pamphlet.

A Study of Assassination.

(A training manual written by the CIA
for distribution to agents and operatives)

He said aloud, 'No shit!'

And as he flicked through it, he gave intermittent 'Wow's, 'Jeez', and an outright, 'I'll be fucked!'

Under the heading *Justification* was:

Murder is not morally justifiable. Assassination can seldom be employed with a clear conscience. Persons who are morally squeamish should not attempt it.

Fenton said: 'You got that right, guys.'

More: *It is desirable that the assassin be transient.*

Then: *Techniques.*

A human being may be killed in many ways…

62

Fenton muttered, 'Oh really?'

The assassin should always be cognisant of one point – 'death' must be absolutely certain.

Call it serendipity or chance, but when Fenton stopped to take his bearings he was outside a sporting goods shop.

Went in.

The music was deafening and he had to recheck it wasn't a disco. No, a sports shop. He asked an assistant, 'What's that noise?'

'It's Heavy D.'

'What?'

'Waterbed Hev.'

'I'm going to have to take yer word for that. Why is it so loud?'

'Most of our clientele are Afro-Americans.'

'You mean black.'

The assistant ignored this and asked what he could do to help. Fenton said, 'I want an old style baseball bat. Not metal or some brilliant new plastic or low fat – the basic slugger. Can you do that?'

Four hundred bucks later, he could.

London

Roberts was determined to tell his wife about the skin cancer. At the very least he'd get laid. So... so it would be a sympathy fuck, but who was counting? All the other ails:

dead bank balance

burnt car

nervous job prospects

he'd leave a bit. No need to tip the balance. He was almost looking forward to dropping his health bombshell. Move him centre stage for a few days.

A *Big Issue* vendor was sporting a spotlessly white T-shirt which declared:

70% of Prostitutes are Convent Educated.

Roberts said, 'What about the other 30%?'

The vendor smiled. 'They're the education.' Argue that.

When he got home he checked quickly to see if his daughter was home.

Nope.

He muttered, 'Thank Christ for that'. Recently she'd been treating him as if he were invisible... no, scratch that – invisible *and* annoying.

His wife said, 'You're home.'

He was going to congratulate her powers of observation, but it wouldn't be a loving start. Instead: 'I have something to tell you.'

She hmphed and said, 'Well, I certainly have something to tell *you*.'

Testily, he snapped, 'Can't it wait?'

'Oh, if your daughter being pregnant isn't a priority then of course it can wait.'

'Jeez… what? I mean, how…?'

'Well darling, I know it's been a while, but if you can't remember how it happens…' And she shrugged her shoulders. He couldn't believe it. Worse, she walked off.

He thought: 'Skin cancer *that.*'

To roost

Stella Davis – Fenton's ex-wife – was loading her washing machine. If she could have known it was the last day of her life, she might have done the wash regardless. It's highly doubtful she'd have added fabric softener.

Her new husband was a teacher and the most stable person she'd ever met. Even his name – Jack Davis – rang of security. A no frills, no shit kinda guy. Jack was yer buddy, the sort of stand up guy who'd have a few beers and slip you a few bucks if you were hurting. When they devised the 'Buddy' system, it was the likes of Jack they envisaged.

Stella didn't love him but, as they say at The Oval, she had a fondness for him. Plus, he was her Green Card, worth a whole shitpile of love and roses.

The love of her life had been The Alien. She came from a family of part time villains:

part of the time they were doing villainy
part of the time they were doing time.

So Fenton's rep was known and admired in her street. It was a mystery to her why it was described as a working class neighbourhood, as few worked. Fenton appeared glamorous and dangerous and all that other good shit that causes fatal love. The biggest hook of all, he was gentle – to, with and about her.

When she got pregnant, he got three years and she woke up. That would be the pattern. He'd be banged up or killed and she decided to start over. Then she miscarried and the loss unhinged her. Near insane with grief and rage, she'd gone to the prison. As he walked into the visiting room, she saw the macho swagger, the hard-eyed hard man and she wanted to wound him.

So, she told him. 'I aborted.'

And he'd gone berserk. Across the table at her and it took six guards to beat him into a stupor if not submission. Perhaps the worst horror was him never uttering a sound.

When Jack Davis showed up, she took him. She'd received one call before she left London from Bill who said, 'Run… for all you're worth.'

She did.

As the machine kicked into overdrive, Stella made some decaff. It was the state of low fat living. She'd been starting to talk American, eg 'carbohydrated'.

The washing was in mega spin and she turned on the radio, it had Star Wars speakers and come-on hyper. It was nostalgia hour and she heard Steeler's Wheel with 'Stuck In The Middle With You'. Oh yeah. With Gerry Rafferty in the line up, they'd been touted as Scotland's answer to Crosby, Stills and Nash, which was pushing the envelope; and then Vince Gill with 'Go Rest High on that Mountain'…

As she'd boarded the plane at Heathrow, a song was playing. Elton John's homage to Princess Diana. Then and now, Stella felt the song that sang it best, that sang it heart-kicked was Vince Gill.

When she heard it, she saw the photo of Di that would wound the soul of the devil himself. It shows her running in a school race at her boys' school. Her face is that of a young girl, trying and eager, and mischievous.

Full of fun.

This whole thing Stella had told to Jack and then played the Gill song.

In a rare moment of insight, he'd said, 'Down those mean streets, a decent song must sometimes go.'

She'd said, 'That's beautiful Jack.'
'No, it's Chandler pastiche.'
'Oh…'

Which bridge to cross
and which bridge to burn.

(Vince Gill)

Brant had to change flights at Dublin. There are no direct flights to Galway in the West of Ireland. He had contacted a long neglected cousin who said he'd meet him on arrival.

Brant asked, 'How will you know me?'

'Aren't you a police man?'

'Ahm… yes.'

'Then I'll know you.'

Brant wanted this crypticism explained but thought it best to leave it alone. Instead, he said, 'So, you're Pat de Brun.'

'Most of the time.'

Brant concluded he was headed for a meet with a comedian or a moron. Probably both.

Brant was already confused by Ireland. At Dublin Airport the first thing he saw was a billboard, proclaiming:

'Costa l'amore per il caffe'

Unless he'd boarded the wrong flight and was now in Rome, it didn't make sense. Shouldn't they be touting tea, or jeez, at the very least, whisky?

His cousin, Pat de Brun, was smiling and Brant's old responses kicked in. 'What's the joke, boyo?'

69

'Tis that you look bewildered.'

And more bewildered he'd get. Pat said, 'You'll be wantin' a drink, or, by the look of ye, the hair of the dog.'

Brant let it go and followed him to the bar. A middle aged woman was tending and declared, 'Isn't the weather fierce?'

Pat ignored the weather report and said, 'Two large Paddies.'

Brant half expected two big navvies to hop on the counter. The drinks came and Pat said,'Slainte.'

'Whatever.'

They took it neat, like men or idiots. It burned a hole in Brant's guts and he went, 'Jesus.'

'Good man, there's a drop of Irish in yah after all.'

'There is now.'

Brant's travel plans were:
1. London to Dublin
2. Dublin to Galway
3. Overnight stay
4. Shannon to America
So far so something.

A tape deck was playing 'Search for the Hero Inside Yourself.' Both men were quietly humming. Brant said, 'Not very Irish is it?'

Pat finished his drink and answered, 'Nothing is anymore. My name is Padraig but there's no way a Brit like yourself could pronounce it.'

The drink was sufficiently potent for Brant to try. He said, 'Pawdrag.'

'Good on yah, that's not bad; but lest I be living on me nerves, let's stick to Pat.'

Brant swallowed. 'Or Paddy.'

Pat de Brun was a distant cousin of Brant. Migration, emigration and sheer poor pronunciation had mutated *de Brun* to *Brant*.

70

Go figure.

Brant was to find Pat a mix of pig ignorance, slyness and humour. If he'd been English, he'd be credited with irony. Apart from sporadic Christmas cards, they were strangers but neither seemed uncomfortable. Course, being half-pissed helped. Brant took out his Weights and offered. It was taken and the bar woman said, 'I could do with a fag myself.'

They ignored her. As Pat blew out his first smoke, he coughed and said, 'Jaysus... coffin nails.'

'Like 'em?'

'I do.'

'Good.'

Envious glances from the woman. But she didn't mind. Men and manners rarely met.

Brant said, 'I better get a move on.'

Pat was truly surprised, asked, 'What's your hurry, where are you going?'

'Well... America... but I better check into a hotel.'

Pat got red in the face... or redder; near shouted, 'There'll be no hotels for the de Bruns! The missus is in Dublin for a few days so you'll be stoppin' with me.'

Brant was tempted, answered, 'If it's no trouble.'

'But of course it's trouble, what's that ever had to do with anything?'

A point Brant felt couldn't be bettered. When the bar woman put them out, she pocketed the cigarettes.

Felicitations

Falls held her breath as the Doctor began to speak. 'Well, Miz… or Miss – I never know the PC term.' And he looked at her. The expression of the misunderstood male run ragged by women's demands.

She wanted to shout, 'Get on with it you moron,' but said tightly, 'Miz is fine.'

'All right, Miz…' And he looked at his notes.

She supplied: 'Falls.'

'Quite so. Well, Miz Falls, you are pregnant. Three months, in fact.'

She was speechless. Now that it was confirmed she felt a burst of happiness and finally said, 'Good!'

If the doctor was expecting this response, he hid it well. 'Ah… when there's, ahm… no *Mr* Falls, one isn't always… pleased.'

'I'm delighted.'

'So I see. Of course, there are alternatives, once the initial euphoria has abated, one might wish for… other options.'

She wanted to smack him in the mouth but said, 'I'm keeping my baby. I am not euphoric, I am, as I said, delighted.'

He waved his hand dismissively like he'd heard this nonsense a hundred times, and said, 'My secretary will advise you of all the details. Good day Miz Falls.' As she was leaving, he said, 'I suppose one ought to say felicitations!'

'You what?'

'It's French for congratulations.'

'Oh, I know what it means, doctor, but I doubt that you do… in any language.'

The secretary typed out all the data and as she handed it over, said, 'Pay no heed to him, he's a toss-pot.'

'Aren't they all?'

A mugging we will go

'Wild, Wild Angels' by Smoky was pouring from a gay bar in the lower reaches of the East Village. A near perfect pop song, it contains all the torch a fading queen could ask for.

The Band-Aiders wanted out of New York and they wanted out now. Josie and Sean O' Brien were the names they were currently using. Their brains were so fucked from chemicals, they weren't sure of anything save their Irish nationality, but years of squatting in south-east London had added a Brixton patois to their accents. Their one surety was they wanted to hit California, and hopefully hit it fucking hard. Sunshine and cults – what could be better?

And wow, had their luck ever held out? First, they broke into Brant's flat and though he'd found and threatened them, they got him first. Next, they murdered a young cop named Tone for his new pants – a pair of smart Farahs. Beaten him to death with a nine wood, not that they were golfers. Golf clubs had replaced baseball bats as the weapon of choice for a brief time in Brixton. Things had returned to normal, though, and bats had now reemerged for walloping the bejaysus outta punters.

That Brant would come a-hunting never occurred to them.

Josie had once been pretty, a colleen near most, blue eyes, pert nose and dirty blonde hair.

But that was well fucked now.

Brixton
squats
sheer viciousness
and of course, every chemical known to boogie had
wrought havoc.

Her hair was now a peroxided yellow, as once touted by
Robbie Williams. Her skin was a riot of spots and sores.
Crack cocaine had given her the perpetual sniffles.

And if *she* was rough, Sean was gone entirely like Sid
Vicious... two years after his death.

They'd got into America as part of a punk band
entourage. They'd then ripped off the band and pawned the
instruments. Now broke, they resorted to what they were –
urban predators. Prey was best from gay bars.

But their amazing run of luck was about to dive.

From the shadows, they watched a group of men on the
sidewalk. Obviously stewed, they were saying goodbyes
with laughter and hugs.

Sean said, 'I'd kill for a cuppa tea.'

'Yeah, gis two sugars wif mine, yah cunt!'

They giggled.

Sean watched as one man broke away, and muttered, 'I'll
give him a good kickin', I will.'

'Yeah, we'll do the bollocks!' Josie felt the rush of adrenalin, the juice kicking into override. She gasped, *'Crank it up
muttah-fuckah!'* Even the boys in the hood would have
admired her accent, not to mention her sentiments.

As the man moved off alone, Sean said, 'Show-time!'

Julian Asche was thirty-five years old. A successful
architect, it had taken him a long time to accept his homo-
sexuality. But New York is a good place to come out. To hear
the women tell it, try finding a guy who *wasn't*:

gay
married
lying
OR

75

all three.

As a seasoned Manhattanite, he'd paid his city dues. Found a way to cohabit with cockroaches, ignore the homeless and be mugged twice. He'd declared, 'Enough already!' and, 'This shit ain't happening to me again!'

Thus, he was left with two choices:

1. Leave
2. Get a gun

He got a gun. Finally, he was a fully fledged commuter. Right down to his Reeboks and war stories. To complete the picture he ate sushi and liked Ingmar Bergman.

The weapon was a Glock. It came to prominence as a terrorist accessory – made mostly of plastic, it got through metal detectors without a bleep. Lightweight, easy to carry and conceal; even the cops took to it. As their no-mention second gun, the true back-up.

Now Josie nudged Sean, said, 'Rock 'n' roll.'

He grunted, added, 'Roadkill.'

They moved.

Their tried and tested method was for Josie to approach the vic and whine, 'Gis a few quid, mate.' Sean then did the biz from the rear. Simple, deadly, effective. It got them Brant, the young copper and one per cent of the Borough of Lambeth. Why change? Indeed.

But Sean did.

Perhaps it was the Rolex. Julian was wearing the Real McCoy. A present from his first lover. So genuine, it looked fake.

Josie did her part, only altering the currency to suit the geography. The song now coming from the bar was Lou Reed's 'Perfect Day'. If fate had a sense of the dramatic, 'Walk On The Wild Side' would have been apt; but it has an agenda, which rarely includes humour, and almost never timing.

The dance began as before. Josie strode up to Julian, whining, 'Gis a few bucks, Mistah.'

Sean, if not exactly the pale rider, pulled rear. For one hilarious moment, Josie's accent confused Julian. He thought she was saying, 'Gis a few fucks Mistah.' He was about to tell her that – 'Gee sister, you sure dialled the wrong number,' when Sean, breaking their routine, went for the Rolex like a magpie on speed. Grabbed for the wrist.

Julian shrugged him off, crying, 'What the...?' Then reached for the Glock in the small of his back. He was a child of the movies, he knew you carried it *above* yer bum. Thus explaining perhaps *'cover yer ass'*. A homophobic would interpret it differently and more crudely. Whatever...

The gun was out, held two handed in Sean's direction. Sean, who'd expected a drunken vic, was enraged, shouted, 'Gimme the watch, yah bollocks!'

Julian shot him in the face. Then the Glock swivelled to Josie and she dropped to her knees, pleading, 'Aw, don't kill me mistah, he made me do it, I swear.'

The CIA responses are hard to beat, that is:

Catholic

Irish

Appalling.

Julian felt the power, the deer kicking the leopard in the nuts. Adrenalined to a new dimension, he asked, 'Tell me, bitch. Tell me why I shouldn't off you. You deserve to be wasted. Go on – *beg* me. Beg me not to squeeze the trigger.'

She begged.

Full frontal

When Brant came too, he'd no idea where he was. What he did know was he was in pain. Ferocious pain. He stirred and realised he was half on the floor, half on the sofa. Still half in the bag. Gradually, it came back:

Ireland
Pat's house
Pub crawling
Quay Street
Dancing Irish jigs.

Dancing! He prayed – 'Please Jesus let me be wrong about the dancing!'

He wasn't.

He was clad in his grey Y-fronts. Not grey by choice but cos he'd washed them white with a blue shirt. Sweat cascaded off his face and he said, 'I'm dying.'

The door opened and Pat breezed in bearing two steaming mugs of tea. 'Howyah, you're wanted on the phone.'

'What?'

'An English fella and by the sound of him a policeman. Likes giving orders.'

'Roberts?'

'That's the lad.'

Lawrence Block in *Even The Wicked*:
'It's a terrible thing,' he said, 'when a man develops a taste for killing.'

78

'You have a taste for it.'

'I have found joy in it,' he allowed. *'It's like the drink, you know. It stirs the blood and quickens the heart. Before you know it, you're dancing.'*

'That's an interesting way to put it.'

Brant gulped the tea and roared, 'Jesus, I'm scalded.'

'Aye, it's hot as Protestants.'

But something else, something that kicked. Pat smiled, said, 'That'll be the hair of the dog.'

'Bloody Rottweiler, was it?'

A moment, as the liquid fought his insides, near lost and Brant got ready to puke. Then lo, it crashed through and began to spread ease.

Pat said, 'Yah better get to the phone.'

Brant said, 'OK,' and thought: 'Ye Gods, I do feel better.'

Roberts said, 'Got you outta bed, did I?'

'Naw, I was playing golf, had to rush in from the ninth.'

'Eh?'

Brant scratched his balls, couldn't believe how better by the minute he was feeling. Maybe he'd never leave Ireland.

Roberts said, 'I had a hell of a job to locate you.'

'I'm undercover.'

'Under the weather, it sounds like. You're not pissed now are you? I mean it's not even ten in the morning.'

'Haven't touched a drop.'

Roberts took a deep breath. He had startling news and he wanted to be startling with it. The plan was to meander, dawdle, and plain procrastinate.

Get to it e…v…e…n…t…u…a…l…l…y.

Like that.

What he said was, 'They've caught the Band-Aiders.'

'Jesus!'

'Yeah.'

Brant wanted to roar:

Where?

79

When?

Who?

Why?

But instead repeated, 'Jesus!'

Roberts figured that counted as 'startled', so he said, 'The deadly duo tried to mug a punter in New York, but guess what?'

Brant had no idea. 'I've no idea.'

'He was carrying a nine millimetre Glock. He must have been influenced by the subway vigilante... what's his name?'

Brant didn't know or care. The healer in the tea had done its job. In fact, he wanted more, more of everything, especially information. 'He killed them?'

'Naw, just the man – the girl begged for her life, and by the time the cops arrived she coughed up everything – stabbing you, killing young Tone... I think she even copped to Lord Lucan and Shergar.'

Brant laughed, this was great. He was truly delighted and thought: 'I love Ireland!' Which, if not logical, was definitely sincere.

Roberts said, 'Now, here's the thing. She's waived extradition and wants to come back. There's one condition though.'

'What? She wants a seat on Concorde or to meet Michael Jackson?'

'Worse. She wants *you* to bring her back.'

Brant couldn't believe it, shouted, 'No, Fuck that! I've plans... I'm going to San Francisco... that's where Fenton is.'

Pat heard the shouting and did the Irish thing. He got Brant more tea and a cigarette. Roberts felt it was time to pull rank and kick some subordinate butt. 'Sergeant, it's not a request. Those on high aren't asking you politely for a favour. It's an order.'

'Shite!'

80

'That too, but look on the bright side – they're springing for it, won't cost you nowt.'

Brant took a hefty slug of the tea, better and bitter, but he wanted to sulk and as he crushed out the cigarette, he whined, 'It's not about the money.'

Roberts laughed out loud. 'Gimme an Irish break. With you it's always about the money.'

It was... *always*.

Brant could hear the shower running and... yes, the sound of Pat singing. Sure enough – 'Search for the Hero Inside Yourself'.

Roberts said, 'Go to the local Garda station in Galway and all the details will be faxed.'

'Fucked, more like. They'll welcome an English policeman, I suppose.'

Roberts was beginning to enjoy this. How often did you get to mess Brant about? His skin cancer was itching like a Hare Krishna and he felt the dehydration beginning. 'Why were they called Band-Aiders? Musicians, were they?'

Brant snorted. 'The only tune they played was from an Oliver Stone film. The guy had a cut on his face and said, "When I'm cut, she bleeds". They both sported snazzy bandages. Cute, eh?'

Roberts couldn't resist it. 'They'll need some bloody bandage to cover what's left of his face.' He wanted suddenly to share his pain about his illness. Brant was the nearest to a friend he had. He began, 'I've been in some pain, Sergeant.'

'Jaysus, who hasn't boyo?'

And he hung up.

Trying to recapture the great moments of the past.

Pat had prepared breakfast as if Man United were expected.

Two plates on the table with:

sausages (2)
eggs (2)
tomatoes (2.5)
fried bread (1)
black pudding (1)

The plates were ample enough for a labour party manifesto.

Brant said, 'Holy shit!'

Pat was already tucking in. 'Get that inside you, man, soak up the booze.'

Odd thing was, Brant was hungry. He sat down, lifted a fork and indicated the black pudding. 'What kind of accident is that?'

'Would you prefer white?'

'White what... eh?'

'It's pudding, the Pope loves it.'

Brant pushed it aside, speared a sausage and said, 'Which tells me what exactly? I mean, the *Pope*... is that a recommendation or a warning?'

Pat laughed, had a wedge of fried bread, said, 'The Pope's a grand maneen.'

'A what?'

'Man-een. In Ireland we put 'een' onto names to make them smaller. By diminishing, we make them accessible. It can be affectionate or mocking, sometimes both.'

Brant found the sausage was good, said, 'This sausage is good... or rather, sausageen.'

'Now you have it. Pour us a drop of tea like a good man.'

They demolished the food and sat back belching. Brant said, 'Lemme get my cigarettes.'

'Don't stir... try an Irish lad.'

He shoved across a green packet with 'MAJOR' in white letters on the front. Brant had to ask. 'Not connected to the bould John I suppose?'

It took a moment to register, then 'Be-god no, these have balls.'

Pat produced a worn Zippo lighter and fired them up. Brant drew deep and near asphyxiated. 'What the fuck?'

'Mighty, eh?'

'Jesus, now I know what they make that pudding from.'

Pat excused himself, saying, 'Gum a less school.' At least that's how it sounded to Brant. It means simply, 'Excuse me'.

Like that.

He came back with the inevitable tea pot and a large white sweater. 'This ganzy is for you. It's an Aran jumper and if you treat it right, it will outlive yer boss.'

Brant never, like *never* got presents; thus he was confused, embarrassed and delighted. 'That's... Jesus... I mean... it's so generous.'

'Tis.'

After Brant had showered, he donned a pair of faded Levis and then the Aran. He loved it, the fit was like poetry. He said, 'I'll never take it off.' Put on a pair of tested Reeboks and he was Action Man.

Pat eyed him carefully, then said, 'Be-god, you're like a Yank.'

'Is that good?'

'Mostly! Mind you, it can also mean, "Give us a tenner".'

Pat volunteered to show him how to find the Gardai. Before leaving, he asked, 'Who's Mayor Mayor?'

Brant was stunned. 'What?'

'Mayor Mayor. You were roaring the name like a banshee last night.'

Brant sat down. 'Gimme one of those coffin nails.' He lit it and felt the tremor in his hand. 'A time back, I had a dog named Mayor Mayor... after a character by Ed McBain.'

Pat didn't have a clue as to who McBain was, but he was Irish and learnt from the cradle not to stop a story with minor quibbles, so said nowt.

Brant was into it, back there, his eyes holding the nine yard stare. 'We had a psycho loose called The Umpire, he was killing the English Cricket Team.'

If Pat had a comment on this, he didn't make it.

'I called him names on TV and he burned my dog, just lit him all to blazes, the dirty bastard.' Brant stopped, afraid his voice would crack.

Pat asked, 'When you caught him, you beat the bejaysus outta him?'

'No.' Very quiet.

'You didn't?' Puzzled.

'We didn't catch him.'

'Pat was truly amazed, muttered, 'I see'. But he didn't.

Brant physically shook himself as if doing so would do the same to his mind. It didn't. 'I loved that dog – he was the mangiest thing you ever saw.' Is it possible to have a smile in a voice? Brant had it now. 'I used to take him for walks up Clapham Common, thought we'd score some women.'

'Did ye?'

'Naw, I was the ugly mutt.' And they both laughed. The tension was easing down, beginning to leak away.

Pat, being Irish, was attuned to loss, pain and bitter-sweet melancholia. 'Lemme tell you a story and then we'll talk no more of sad things. Tell me, did you ever hear of the word "bronach"?'

'Bron… what?'

'You didn't. OK, it's the Gaelic for sadness, but be-god, it's more than that, it's a wound in the very soul.' Pat paused to light a cigarette and sip some tea. He knew all about timing. 'Our eldest lad, Sean… a wild devil. He'd build a nest in yer ear and charge you rent. I loved him more than sunlight. When he was eight he caught a fever and died. There isn't a day goes by I don't talk to him. I miss him every minute I take breath. Worst, odd times I forget him, but I don't beat myself up for that – it's life… in all its granite hardness. The point I'm hoping to make – and eventually I'll get there – is life is terrible, and the trick is not to let it make you a terror. Now, there's an end to it. C'mon, I'll bring you to the Garda.'

Brant couldn't decide if it was the wisest thing he'd ever heard or just a crock. As he rose he decided he'd probably never be sure; said, 'Pat, you're a maneen.'

Cast(e)

Falls was in the canteen eating dry toast, no butter; drinking milk, no taste. Rosie, her friend, breezed in. As much as you can breeze if your arm's in a sling and your face is bruised.

'Hiya Rosie.'

'Hiya hon.'

Like that.

Rosie said, 'Yer wondering what happened to me, right?'

'Ahm...'

'Falls – look at me! I'm a wreck.'

Falls put the toast down. 'Oh my God! What have you been doing, girl?'

'Didn't you know I was on holiday? Jack and I've been saving to go to India, and we went.'

Falls couldn't resist. 'And they didn't like you much.'

Rosie reached over, touched her friend's arm. 'Wake up and smell the coffee honey, OK? I've always wanted to go to Goa cos of the old hippy trail and those beaches...' Her arms and face were tan; what's known as a cowboy tan – the body stays soap-white.

Falls tried to focus. 'Did you have a terrific time?'

'I can't believe you don't know! We flew to Delhi and got a cab at the airport. The taxis, they drive like the worst night in Brixton... sorry... I mean...'

Falls being black, didn't take it personally. When white Londoners reached for adjectives, metaphors for chaos, they used Brixton. If hardly commendable, it was vague

86

times comprehensible. So it goes, an urban blues.

Rosie, less fired, said, 'A transit van hit us, driven by Australians. The taxi driver was killed and I was unconscious for five days.'

Falls, for an instant, near forgot the child she carried and touched her friend's face. 'Ah darlin', are you all right?'

'I am now. They pinned my arm, and do you know, they don't bind broken ribs? They hurt like a son-of-a-bitch. Jack, the rascal...'

'Rascal? Have you been watching Sean Bean in Sharpe?'

Rosie laughed. She had a reach down in your gut laugh with her heart – and screw the face lines. 'He never got a scratch. I had concussion and the doctor said, "Your head won't be right for some time." The wanker. I'm a WPC – my head will never be right! But enough about me, fascinating though it is. What's with you, girl? You're distant.'

Falls let her eyes drop to her stomach and edged a tiny smile lit with mischief, wonder, delight.

Rosie stared, eyes like saucers, and then, *'Oh my word! Oh... oh... oh!'* And jumped up, trying to hug Falls with her good arm. The various cops in the canteen turned round, their look proclaiming: *What the hell is it with these women?*

Rosie touched her head, looked bashful as well as bashed, said, 'Sorry,' then whispered,

'Congratulations... oh, I love you.'

So all in all, it has to be said, Rosie sure received the news a whole lot better than the doctor. Trying to keep her voice low, she asked, 'How does it feel? Are you having morning sickness?'

'No, nothing; but I think I'm going to get my wish.'

'What?'

'Huge boobs.'

Their attempts to stifle the laughter only made it worse. Then Falls told her of the arsonist and how Brant was away. 'Don't you see? It's my chance. If I catch the guy I'll get promotion and be able to afford the baby bills.'

Rosie shook her head. 'Don't be crazy, the guy could be dangerous.'

'He's all mouth, no danger.'

But she was wrong.

The duty sergeant appeared, said, 'If comedy hour is over, I have a case that requires female tact.' Which told them exactly zero.

On the way, Falls said 'If it's a girl, I'll call her Rosie.'

An elderly woman was sitting in the interview room. Falls sat and checked the charge sheet. The woman leant over, peered and said, 'Good Lord, you're a black person!'

Falls geared up. 'Is that a problem?'

'Oh no dear. It's nice they're letting you people in. I love Ray Charles.'

The charge sheet was, as usual, unhelpful, so Falls said, 'Mrs Clark... Why don't you tell me in your own words what happened?'

She was happy to.

'I was sitting in Kennington Park – so nice there – and a man walked up to me and just stood there. So I said, "Can I help you?" and he said, "Look, look – I'm exposing myself!" He sounded very agitated.'

'Was he?'

'Was he what, my dear?'

'Flashing... I mean, did he... take out his privates?'

'His John Thomas, you mean? I said – "You'll have to move closer as my eyesight is poorly".'

Falls tried to contain herself, asked, 'What happened?'

'He moved closer and I stabbed it with my Papermate. That's when he started screaming and the police came.'

Falls wanted to hug her. 'Would you like some tea?'

'Oh yes please, dear. Two sugars and a Marietta. Just one, I don't want to spoil my dinner.' As Falls stood up, the woman added, 'You're so kind, dear. Might I ask you a question?'

'Of course.'

'Your tribe, the coloureds – why do they wear those caps the wrong way round?'

'It's fashion, Ma'am.'

'I think it's rather silly, but… if it keeps you happy…' Then she added, 'I hate to be a nuisance but will I be able to get my Papermate back?'

The American way

The Alien walked into a Seattle coffee place. He'd always wanted to say, 'Hi, how you doin'? My usual… half-caff decaff triple Grande caramel cappuccino with wings…'

And of course, the chick'd say, 'You're British, right?'

Instead he said, 'Espresso please.' Got that and a wedge of Danish, went to check the phone directory.

Bingo .

There she was, under the name Bill had given him. Jotted down the address and bit into the Danish. Too sweet. The sports bag was at his feet and the shape of the bat was barely discernible.

Stella, the Alien's ex-wife, had snuck a cigarette. In America now they don't frown on smoking they just out and out shoot you. Her last trip home, unbeknownst to Jack, she'd bought a carton. Rothmans. In all their deadly glory. They'd come with a free T-shirt which shrunk in the wash. Size XL, a few more spins, it would fit a person.

Cracking the cellophane, she opened a fresh pack and lit up with the kitchen matches.

Ah… Dinner was in the oven and she'd have time to use air fresheners before Jack got home, add a splash of Patchouli.

Who's smoking?

Her mother regularly sent Liptons tea and the South

London Press. Jack would say, 'You English and your tea!'
Loving it, loving she was English and stressed it. When Jack
got home she made him a dry martini, very dry and with
two olives. It was a ritual. He'd say, 'Two?'

'Cos I love you too much.'

Like that.

Then, 'Something smells good.'

'It's your favourite.'

'Meatloaf?'

'You betcha.'

When he'd first asked for it, she thought he meant 'Bat
Out Of Hell'. She was still English then. Now she had to
work at it. It wasn't that she ever felt American, but she had
the moves.

Then he hugged her and she got a blast of Tommy
Hilfiger. For one fleeting moment she remembered Brut and
Fenton, but let it slide, not even li̇ ƺer… just keep on
moving, like a song you can't recall.

So that was how it was when Jack got home. After the
meatloaf, the doorbell went and Jack moved to answer.

A voice said, 'Package for Stella.'

As he opened the door, he was still half turned to her, a
huge smile making him look boyish. Fenton said, 'One!'

And slammed the bat into Jack's stomach.

'Two!'

Upended it and drove the top against Jack's chin, the
bone splintering into his brain.

'Chun!'

And he beamed at Stella, asked, 'Howzat, darlin'?'

She was holding the dinner plates, too frozen to drop
them.

Fenton kicked the door shut.

'Guess Who's Coming to Dinner…? And blacker than
you can begin to imagine.'

> 'We were somewhere around Barstow on the edge of the desert when the drugs began to take hold.'
>
> (Opening lines of 'Fear and Loathing in Las Vegas')

'You're a cute hoor,' said Pat.

'What?'

'The way you handled them cops at the station. Jaysus, they were eating outta yer hand. When did a policeman ever offer a cup o' tea? I'll never get over the bate of that ... As I said, *glic*.'

'Click?'

'It's the same as cute hoor, but slyer.'

'But it's a compliment?'

'Is it?'

They were in The Quays pub on Quay Street. Lest you forgot, it said so above the door. Pat had told Brant that Brad Pitt had been in and that, 'No more than Geldof, he was a bit shy of the soap 'n' water.'

Brant exclaimed, 'You can be one vicious bastard, you know!'

'Ary, I'm only coddin'.'

Brant had come to Ireland for all sorts of reasons and curiosity was probably the best he'd articulated. Getting laid never came into it, but lo and behold, he was about to.

They were drinking slow bottles of Guinness and Pat said, 'There's a wan over there has an eye for you.'

'What?'

'She has a mighty chest on her and a bit o' mileage, but for all that…'

'What are you on about?'

Pat moved back from the bar, gave Brant the full Irish appraisal, then said, 'I'd say you're a holy terror for the women.' And then he stepped over to the woman, had a few words and returned. 'She thanks you kindly and a glass of sweet sherry would be grand.'

Brant took a look, not bad at all. A touch of the Margo Kidders… well, OK – Margo's mother, but in prime shape. Course, the fact that she fancied Brant gave her bonus points all over the shop.

As Brant ordered, Pat said, ''Tis what Connemara men do for penance.'

Yet again, Brant had no idea what he meant and dreaded trotting out, 'What?' yet again. What he'd do, he'd get two small cards printed,

1. Yellow
2. Red

Write in small letters 'What?' on the first, then 'WOT?' on the second. Jaysus, they'd think he was deaf. Scratch that. So he said, 'What?' And threw in, 'Excuse me?' for colour.

'Connamara men, they drink sherry as penance.' The sherry was placed on the counter and Pat said, 'Well, go on, man, she can hardly whistle for it.'

He brought it over, said wittily, 'Hi.'

She laughed and said, 'I can see I'm not going to get a word in edgeways.'

'What?'

'Sit down there, you big lump – I'm Sheila.'

A while later, Pat came over, said, 'I've lost me friggin' lighter.'

'The Zippo?'

93

'Aye, blast it to hell, it had "1968" on the front.'
Sheila said, 'Ask St Anthony.'
And Brant said, 'Ask him what?'
Pat and Sheila loved that.

'I have long known that it is part of God's plan for me to spend a little time with each of the most stupid people on earth.'

(Bill Bryson)

When Falls met the snitch in the place he'd selected, she remembered a description from Karon Hall's 'Dark Debts'.

'If you didn't have a gun going in,
they'd provide one at the door.'

At the rear of the Cricketers, near The Oval, it was a dive. Falls arrived first and nodded to the barman. A big guy with

red shirt
red jeans
red face

She resisted the impulse to say, 'Hi, Red.'

He said, 'You sure you got the right place?'

'I'm sure.'

'We don't get many chicks, is all.'

Chicks!

'Well I'm sure once the word on the ambiance gets out, you'll be stampeded.'

Leigh came in, immediately looked angry and pushed her to a back table demanding, 'Why were you talking to him?'

'It's against the rules?'

'You're not supposed to draw attention.'

'Well, there was me 'n' him – did you expect me to hide?'

'People talk, you know.'

He then jumped up, had a word with Red and came back with two glasses of a greenish tint, pushed one at her, said, 'It's lime cordial.'

And I'm supposed to do what with it exactly?'

Leigh was getting seriously upset. 'It's for cover.'

'Oh I see, we lurk behind them.'

'Mr Brant was never like this.'

Falls felt they'd done enough pleasantries, time to jerk the leash. 'You're a stupid person, but that's OK. What I need is fairly simple. You tell me and I'm outta here. There's an arsonist, recent of Croydon, and I need to know where he hangs.'

Leigh began moving his glass, the colour didn't improve. 'You don't want to be messing with that piece of work.'

Falls sighed then clamped her hand on his knee. 'Where?'

'You're not playing by the rules, it has to be drawn out.'

She pinched hard and he jumped. She hissed, 'Leigh, there are no rules… *where*?'

'The snooker hall at The Elephant. Thinks he's Paul Newman in *The Hustler*… He's there all day.'

She released her grip, rooted in her bag and then palmed him a twenty. He was indignant. 'This is supposed to buy me what? It wouldn't pay me light bill for a week!'

Now she smiled, said, 'I dunno, you could always hop up there, get us a few more of these drinks… oh, sorry – *disguises*.'

On her way out, she ignored Red and it seemed to be what he expected.

> 'The best the white world
> offered was not enough
> ecstasy for me. Not enough
> life, joy, kicks, darkness,
> music; not enough night.

(Jack Kerouac)

As Fenton tried not to run, he felt the adrenalin build to a point beyond mere rush. His mind roared: *You did it, you did it, you bloody did it!* — Then his arm was grabbed. Disbelief pounded through his body.

Caught! Already!

And turned to see a black guy, something familiar about him, the guy saying, 'Yo, fool, you owes me a buck and a half!'

'What?'

'The other day, dude. I be giving yo' sorry ass a pamphlet 'bout dem CIA…'

'Oh right… I thought it was free.'

'Where yo' been, dude? Ain't nothing free on the street.'

Fenton reached for change, handed over a five. The guy wailin', 'What cha thinkin', like I'm gonna make change?'

Fenton laughed, said, 'Keep it, knock yourself out mate.'

'Yo dissin' me man, dat what cha thinkin'?'

Now the Alien laughed out loud, asked, 'Is that what they're calling it? Dissin'. What will you guys think of next?'

Close call

The Super had summoned Roberts.

These meetings were never warm; it usually meant a bollocking. When Roberts came in the Super was dunking a biscuit in tea, said, 'Hurry up, man, shut the door.'

He didn't offer tea or a seat; got to it. 'I've had a call from across the water.'

Roberts wondered – from Ireland? ... Brant? ... No. Even he couldn't be that drunk – and said neutrally, 'Yes, sir?'

'From Noo Yawk.'

Pronounced it thus to demonstrate he could be a kidder or simply an asshole; continued: 'There's been a murder – two murders – in San Francisco.'

Roberts wanted to say, *only two*?

The Super brushed crumbs from his splendid uniform, noisily finished the tea. Can tea be chewed? He was giving it a good try.

'Reason they called us is the woman is a Londoner.' He consulted his notes. 'A Stella Davis, but originally Stella Fenton. Ring any bells?'

'Uh-oh.'

'Is that an answer?'

'Reg Fenton, "The Alien"... Did he use a bat?'

The Super was impressed, if a tiny bit miffed. Had to check the notes, then confirmed, 'By Jove, you're right. They expect he'll head for home, so notify the airport chappies.'

'Yes, sir... How did they know it was him...I mean... so quickly?'

'He left the bat.'

✝ ✝ ✝

Falls was a touch surprised that Leigh's information was correct. She went to the snooker hall in the late afternoon. Round three, in there.

She'd been expecting a tide of looks and remarks.

Lone woman in the last male bastion.

Lone black woman.

But there wasn't, as the place was empty.

It was situated above a tailors with the sign 'ESPOKE'.

It puzzled her till she realised the 'B' had done a Burton, so to speak. Up two flights of badly lit stairs and she knew, in her condition, it wouldn't be long till she wouldn't be able to do that. The baby was beyond joy, it was up there in the realm of ecstasy.

A toilet flushed and out emerged the suspect. He didn't seem surprised to see her, asked, 'Fancy a quick game?'

'Some other time.'

He was smiling. 'On yer lonesome this trip?'

'Am I going to need help?' She kept it light – let's all stay nice 'n' loose – relaxed, even.

He spread both hands on the table, said, 'No way, babe.'

Falls moved a little closer. 'If you could spare me a short time to come to the station, clear up a small situation.'

He was running his hand idly over the snooker balls, exclaimed, 'What? Now?'

'If you wouldn't mind, it would be a great help.'

Now he had the black ball in his right hand, fisting it. 'You speak well for a nigger, almost like a white bitch. That what you want, to be white, eh?'

She took a deep breath.

He shouted, 'Black in right centre pocket!' and flung it in

her face. Caught her full impact on the forehead and she staggered back, felt her knees buckle. Then he was dragging her by
the hair, saying, 'I keep telling them, put-out-the-trash.'

And he dragged her through the doors, paused, then
slung her, roaring, 'Black on the way out!'

'Yada Yada'
or some such

(Melanie)

B rant was sitting in the GBC – a restaurant right in the centre of Galway. It had the mentality and kudos of a transport caff, ie lashings of food, *good* food, cheap and friendly. Brant liked it a lot.

A waitress asked, 'By yourself, are you?'

'What?… Oh yeah… No. My cousin's coming.'

And caught himself, thought — 'What am I doing? Jeez, I'll be telling her the size of me socks next.'

He gave a mortified smile and she said, 'T'will be nice for ye.'

Argue that.

Brant recalled the night before and Sheila. She had a small flat along the canal, and no sooner there, than she hopped on him. Gave him a ferocious ride. He'd lain back on the floor, exclaimed, 'Wow, that was Trojan!'

'You mean you're done?'

'Jeez, woman – one shag and I'm for a kip!'

She'd given him an elbow in the ribs, said, 'Ary go on outta that! Two squirts and you're calling it a night! I'll get you roaring till the small hours.'

She did and did, till them small hours. Finally he cried, 'I'll give you serious money not to touch me dick again.'

She laughed out loud and climbed on. When finally

she'd nodded off, he'd limped to his feet and hobbled outta there as fast as he could manage.

Pat arrived in. 'There you are… Sheila's looking for you.'

When he saw Brant's alarm, he added, 'Only coddin' yah! Isn't she a gas woman?'

'Gas?'

'She's a widow, you know.'

'Christ, I believe it! I'm only surprised she's at large.'

Pat shouted across the tables, 'Mary, bring us a nice cuppa tea and a currant bun, there's a good girl.' He sat down, said, 'So you'll be going now?'

'Yeah, the local boyos are running me down to Shannon… see me off the premises, I suppose.'

Pat looked sad. 'I'll be sorry to see you go.'

Brant reached in his pocket, produced a fancy bag with 'WILLIAM FALLER' written in gold across it. 'I didn't know what else to get.'

Pat opened it fast and out fell a shining gold Zippo. He turned it over, the inscription: 'PATEEN'. Pat said, 'I'll mind it like laughter.'

'In south-east London we're not big on hugs or that, so I'll…'

Pat got up and grabbed him in a hug that Sheila would have admired, said, 'You be careful now, young Brant.'

On the way to Shannon, Brant reached for a cigarette and lit it carefully with a Zippo. His thumb near covered the '1968'.

Each angel is terrible

(Rilke)

Heading for Mexico and aiming specifically for Acapulco was a tropical depression. Very soon, as it gathered force, ferocity and momentum, it would be upgraded to hurricane status and, of course, named. As usual, despite the feminists, it would be called Pauline. They were sure going to remember her.

The Mexican President, Ernesto Zedillo, was assured it was not a serious storm and yes, go ahead with his trip to Germany.

He did.

It would be a tragedy of huge human loss but also bring about a major political crisis.

Fenton boarded his plane and felt he should at the very least have one of those hats so beloved of British resorts, with the logo: 'KISS ME QUICK'.

He remembered an awful Elvis movie with Ann-Margret or one of those Elvis-type movie women... lush bodied... Now what the hell is the name of it?

As the seat belt sign flashed in preparation for take off, it came to him and he muttered,'Yeah, *Fun in Acapulco*.'

Now try to get the damn tune out of his head as it lodged there like stale muesli.

Brown is the new Black

(London fashion guide)

Nancy D'Agostino didn't want her assignment. Like sure, nurse-maiding some English bobby. He'd probably smoke a pipe and wear one of those London Fog godawful raincoats.

She looked like Nancy Allen. Remember her? A real cutesy who'd been married to John Carpenter before he lost the run of himself and donated his talent to Wes Craven. She'd been at her prettiest in *Carrie* and her slide began post *Philadelphia Experience*.

Nancy held a placard — 'D S BRANT LONDON' — and figured even an English cop could detect this.

As Brant emerged from Immigration, he spotted Nancy and saw her smile. He thought, 'Jaysus, I'm going to get a jump on this side of the Atlantic too.'

He was wearing the Aran sweater and blue serge trousers. Nancy thought, 'Oh my God, one of the Clancy Brothers.'

Brant looked round. 'Jaysus, it's busy.'

Nancy produced her ID. 'I'm Sergeant D'Agostini with the New York City Police Department. I'll be your guide and facilitator while you're here.'

'Facil-i-what?'

She took a deep breath and before she could speak, he slapped her thigh, said, 'Lighten up, woman. Where's the bar?' And he produced a cigarette.

She put out her hands. 'This is a NO SMOKING zone.'

He eyeballed her and cranked a worn Zippo. 'Are we cops or what?'

'Well yes, but…'

'So fuck 'em. Let's get a brewski.'

The bar at JFK is a good intro to New York. The staff are rude

busy

hostile.

After Brant and Nancy had waited for five minutes, she said, 'Let's head into Manhattan, we'll get you a cold one at your hotel.'

Brant gave his satanic smile, roared, 'Hey Elvis, before Labour Day, all right?'

Nancy had to suppress a smile – he sounded so Noo Yawk. The barman asked, 'What'll it be?'

'Coupla beers.'

'Domestic or imported?'

Brant leant on the counter, still smiling, right in the guy's face. 'Forgot the floss eh? … Bring us two strong beers and bring 'em now.'

Nancy asked, 'This isn't your first time in America?'

He reached in his pocket, showed her a small book:

Asshole's Guide To New York – How To Be Ruder Than The Natives.

(By P Catherine Kennedy)

Brant asked, 'You want a glass?' And he chugged his from the bottle.

She said, 'Like I have a choice.'

He ruffled her carefully brushed hair. 'I think you're my kinda chick.'

Children's program

Deep down in an area beyond definition, Falls struggled to wake. She knew consciousness was reachable but she couldn't make the first step. The plans for the baby, how they'd curl up together on the couch and watch TV... If she could recall the names of the Teletubbies, she felt she'd crash to the surface. Tinky-Winky. OK. Got one. That's the blue colour, and... Dipsy. Oh yeah. On a roll now. The yellow one – what was the little shit's name? ... Da-da? ... No, but close. ... La-La! Yes! Just the fourth to go. The small red fella... with the simplest name of all. She was that near and then it began to slip. With stark terror she forgot what she was trying to remember, saw a black meteorite come hurtling and tried to shout... Dougal... Magic Roun...

And her mind shut down.

✝

A radio was playing softly in the hospital ward. Rosie prayed that Falls couldn't hear the particular song now playing – Toni Braxton with Kenny G – 'An Angel broke My Heart'.

Jesus.

She sat by her friend's side holding her hand. The nurse came, did nurse-like things like fluffing the pillow, checking her watch, sighing.

Rosie asked, 'Will she wake up?'

'You'd have to speak to her doctor.'

'What can I do?'

'Talk to her.'

'Can she hear me? … Or have I to speak to her doctor?'

The nurse gave her trained smile, alight with:

understanding

tolerance

and the tiniest hint of contempt .

'Just chat like you would ordinarily.'

After the nurse left, Rosie muttered, 'Cow,' then cleared her throat self-consciously, as if she were recording. Hesitantly she began, 'So hon… Good grief, I nearly asked how you were.'

She glanced round to check if her faux pas had been clocked, then, 'Where was I? … I never got to tell you about my trip to Goa. Oh yeah, Jack was always on about the sanitation and he couldn't see any evidence of pipes. Me? … All I need to know is it works, like pur-leeze, spare me the mechanics. But then someone said, "Notice all the pigs?" They were everywhere and very well fed.' (Rosie gave a small shriek) — You've guessed it! Isn't it too awful? I'll never eat a bacon butty again.'

Then Rosie felt a pang of hunger. She was on yet another diet, the 'T' model.

T for torture.

She could murder an obscenely over-buttered thick wedge of toast, coat the lot in marmalade and eat it without dignity so the juice ran down her chin … and she'd wash the lot down with sugared tea.

Ah!

Yet again she felt tears for Falls, for herself, for carbohydrated freedom. Then she straightened her back, said, 'Hon, I have a confession to make. I'd never have told you, but I fancied the pants off yer fella. Not that I'd ever have… you know, but he sure had something. That cute bum… but it

107

was those staring eyes. I thought he could see into my soul. Isn't that daft? He made me feel so exposed I had to look away.'

Falls stirred and Rosie jumped. But it was only a reflex and she settled back into the void. Rosie continued to hold her hand.

✝

Roberts was beginning to wear out a space in front of the Super's desk. As usual, he was getting a bollocking. The Super tore into him about the usual fuck ups, then asked, 'What's the story on the ducks?'

For an insane moment, Roberts thought he said, 'What's the story on the ducks,' and wondered if the radiation was softening his brain. He answered, 'Excuse me?'

'The ducks in Hyde Park, some nutter beheaded five of them.'

Roberts was sore tempted to try, 'Not our side of the pond,' but went with, 'How is it our concern, sir?'

'How? I'll tell you flamin' how... the heads were put through the letter box of the Chief Constable at his place in Old Town Clapham. What do you say to that?'

Again the demons urged – *'Duck!'* – but without waiting for a reply, the Super was thundering further. 'As for the WPC... Forbes...'

'Falls, sir.'

'Eh?'

'Her name, sir, it's Falls.'

'Don't get impertinent laddie. Do we have any hope of apprehending them or have they joined the migration to America?'

Roberts thought that was quite witty and probably true but he said, 'We're following a definite line of inquiry.'

The Super was out of his chair, shouting, 'In other words, we haven't the foggiest.'

108

But Roberts did have a definite lead. Following the oldest police hunch of all, he got back to the beginning. Roberts had checked with Croydon CID. Sure enough the suspect had bolted for home. That anyone would flee *to* Croydon was a measure of how desperate he was. The buzz had hit the station that his whereabouts were known. Eager constables flocked to Roberts hoping to be part of the team. He was having none of it. Outside the station, a Volvo was waiting, engine turning, door open. Roberts peered in. 'You're keen, I'll give you that.'

The driver, a blond haired man in his twenties smiled, asked, 'Croydon?'

Roberts got in. 'What's yer name sonny?'

'McDonald, Guv.'

'Oh wonderful, a bloody Scot. Spare me the Billy Connolly shite, OK?'

McDonald put the car in gear, asked blankly, 'Billy who?'

'Good lad, you'll go far.'

Elgin Lane is that rarity in this part of London. It's got trees and grass verges and a large Greek presence. No connection to them marbles.

McDonald parked and Roberts said, 'Number nine.'

They got out and walked casually to the house. A line of bells, reading: Zacharopolous / Ohrtanopolous Yoganopolous.

Like that.

Except for one blank bell, indicating the ground floor. Roberts said, 'Use all yer police training and guess which one is our man.'

The door was ajar and in they went, scrutinised the ground floor flat. Roberts said, 'Tut tut, no dead bolt, just yer basic Yale… what do you weigh, son?'

'Weigh?'

'It's not a difficult question.'

'Fourteen stone.'

'Well son, the door won't come to us.'

'Oh.'

'Right.'

McDonald braced himself against the far wall and before he launched, a young woman came down the stairs, gave Roberts a dazzling smile and said, 'Kalimera.'

Roberts answered,'Whatever,' and after she left, added, 'The Greeks have a word for it all right... OK son, are you going to hang about all day?'

He wasn't and took the whole jam of the door in his onslaught.

Roberts gave a low whistle. 'What are they feeding them?' And followed in.

The police piled down a small corridor, which translates as Sweeney tactics. Roar like bulls, pound them boots, and put the shite crossways in all and sundry.

The suspect was crashed out on a double bed, entangled in a sheet. He was arse naked. A dense cloud of 'hash-over' near made him invisible. Despite the noise, he didn't stir.

Roberts asked, 'What is that smell?'

'Dope, sir.'

'And there's the biggest dope of all. Go get a jug of cold water – *very* cold water.'

'Yes, sir.'

McDonald returned with a large basin, it made a clinking sound. 'On the rocks.'

'Perfect, the Chief Constable will be looking over his shoulder.'

McDonald already knew that. 'Shall I?'

'Give it yer best, lad.'

McDonald swung the basin in a wide arc and on the upward tilt, he let the contents fly.

Whoosh!

A ferocious roar came from the bed and the suspect leapt up, crying, 'What's happening, man?'

Roberts said, 'Wakey, wakey,' and nodded to McDonald.

110

He moved quickly and catching the sus by the hair, flipped him over and handcuffed him, hands behind the back. He considered, then open handed he gave the sus an almighty slap on the arse.

Roberts gave a low laugh and the sus tilted his head round. If he was cowed, he wasn't showing it. 'Hey, where's the black cunt – ain't she doing house calls no more?'

McDonald raised his hand but Roberts signalled no. Emboldened, the sus taunted, 'What is this anyway? I haven't got a TV licence... that it?'

Roberts glanced at the TV, then casually tipped it over. 'No TV either. OK... let's go.'

McDonald dragged the sus to his feet, wrapped a blanket round him and pushed him forward.

The sus shouted, 'Ey! lemme get the Tamogotchi!'

Roberts was puzzled. 'You want a takeaway now?'

McDonald stifled a laugh. 'It's a toy, sir, a cyber pet.'

The sus looked at McDonald almost warmly as if he'd found an ally, said, 'Yeah mate, I'm going for the record. I've kept it alive for twenty days already.'

Roberts asked, 'Where is it?'

The sus was animated now. 'Under the pillow, man, you got to keep it near – it gets lonely.'

Roberts looked at McDonald, said, 'Well, Constable, you know what to do.'

McDonald got the pet and glanced briefly at it. The sus said, 'Give it here, dude.'

McDonald dropped it, then lifted his foot and crushed it with his heel.

A howl of anguish went up.

Roberts felt he might have found a replacement for Brant.

'One of the most disturbing facts that
came out in the Eichman trial was that
a psychiatrist examined him and
pronounced him perfectly sane.
We equate sanity with a sense of
justice, with humanness, with the
capacity to love and understand people.
We rely on the sane people of the
world. And now it begins to dawn on us
that it is precisely the sane ones who
are the most dangerous.'

— Thomas Merton.

Fenton liked Mexico. Well, he liked Acapulco in so far
as it was hot and sleazy. And boy was it hot, was it
ever?

From early morning that heat just rolled up and smacked
you in the face.

A sucker punch.

He was staying at El Acapulco and, wow, how did they
come up with that? El?

Lounging by the pool, he signalled a waiter.

'Si, Senor?'

This was great, like being in a John Wayne movie. Fenton
had, like tops, ten Spanish words and decided to spend a

112

few now. Tried: 'Donde esta la Rio Grande?'

'Senor?'

'Just pulling yer chain mate.' He held up two fingers and said, 'Dos Don Equis.'

'Si, Senor.'

Fenton stretched and then read what he'd so far composed.

SILHOUETTES
So Sharp the budding hope – a flicker
lone your face
this night a past remember
can you some the dread took on
this silhouetted
this justified alone…

That's it. That's what he had.

Once he'd heard David Bowie interviewed. What the spiderman did was, write all the lines down, then cut them up with a scissors and let 'em scatter on the floor. Then he'd pick them up haphazardly and that'd be the shape.

The beers came, silver tray 'n' all. The waiter was about to pour when Fenton shouted, 'Jeez, Jose, don't do that! Yah friggin wet-back, don't yah know shit, yah spic bastard?'

Fenton had seen the change from glasses to bottles. No one used a glass no more. Just took that beer by the neck, chugged it cool.

Posing.

Oh sure, but what the fuck – he could nod towards cool. Plus, he really liked the way the moisture drops slid down the bottle, like pity.

He looked at the waiter who was standing perplexed and said, 'Yo, Jose, get with the game, vamoos caballero,' and laughed. He was having a high old time. The waiter, whose name was Gomez, went back to the bar and said, 'That animal needs taming.'

113

If you'd leant on the precise translation, you'd get the exact sense of 'gringo' to suggest 'Alien'.

Hurricane Pauline was building, moving closer.

My kind of town

(Ol' Blue Eyes)

Nancy D'Agostine had arranged accommodation in Kips Bay on East 33rd for Brant. He looked at her. 'Run the name by me again.'

'East 33rd?'

'Jaysus… the other bit.'

'Oh… Kips Bay.'

'Screw that babe, I'm for The Village.'

'But it's been arranged by the Department.'

Brant gave her his full smile, said, 'Fuck 'em, eh? I want to stay in a 'Y' in The Village.'

She looked for an exit on the ramp and thought, 'Could be worse – he might have had a hard-on for The Bronx, and then what?'

Brant watched her drive and asked, 'This is an automatic?'

'Yes.'

'Stick-shift?'

'What?'

'Four wheel drive?'

She glanced at him and he slapped her knee. 'Just winding yah up, babe.'

Gritting her teeth, she said, 'I'm a sergeant in Homicide… do you have any idea of what it takes to make detective, to get my shield?'

Brant said, 'It takes a babe… am I right?'

115

The Band-Aider, Josie O'Brien as she was now officially identified, was being held in the psycho ward. 'Why?' asked Brant.

Nancy gave the department answer. 'Suicide watch.'

Brant gave an ugly snort. 'She kills other people – not a snowball's chance of her hurting herself.'

Nancy agreed but continued, 'She saw her boyfriend shot in the face and had to beg for her own life… she could slip into depression.'

Brant shook his head, then asked, 'So… can I see her?'

Incarceration had suited Josie. Being off the streets, a bath, nutrition, had transformed her. Her dirty blond hair was now shining and looked high-lighted. The previously scabbed, worn face was now scrubbed clean and her eyes had a sparkle.

As Brant prepared to enter the room, he turned to Nancy. 'Where are you going?'

'I'm to be present. It's…'

'Department Regulations. Christ, will yah learn a new tune? Look, I'll buy yah dinner if yah fuck off for ten minutes.'

Nancy, who thought she'd gotten some sort of handle on Brant, asked, 'Ever hear of Popeye Doyle?'

'Nope.'

'That figures. Get it straight, I'm with you all the way.'

Brant decided to roll with it, said, 'Yah dirty article.'

When Brant walked into the room, Josie appeared almost shy. On their previous meeting, her partner had sunk a knife in Brant's back. She said, 'Hiya.'

He didn't answer, took the chair on the other side of the table. The hospital guard gave Nancy an expectant look, like, *what's going down?*

She had no idea.

Brant reached in his pocket and everybody jumped. He took out his Weights and Zippo, placed them on the table.

116

The guard said, 'This is a NO SMOKING ZONE,' as if noticing him for the first time.

Brant gave him a brief glance. 'Fuck off.'

Nancy signalled to the guard – 'Cool it'. He tried.

Brant tapped the cigs. 'Want one?'

'Oh, yes please.'

He shook two free and Josie took one. As he cranked the Zippo, he seized her wrist, the flame in her face, asked, 'Why'd ya kill the young copper?'

If Josie was spooked, she stifled it. 'Gis a cup o' tea, cunt.'

Brant let her go and asked, 'What's she on?'

Nancy looked to the guard, 'The methadone program.'

Brant shrugged, asked Josie, 'Why'd you want to go back?'

'I'm homesick.'

He laughed out loud and she added, 'I'm going to be in a mini-series, maybe Winona Ryder will play me. I'd let Brad Pitt play Sean.'

Brant played along, 'Gonna be famous, that it?'

'I've got an agent.'

'You've got a hell of an imagination. You're going to Holloway, not Hollywood. The only stars you'll see are when the bull dykes ram yer head against the bars.'

Josie looked to Nancy, panic writ large. 'Tell him to shut his mouth!'

Brant stood up. 'When can I have her?'

Nancy consulted the paperwork. 'She's waived all extradition, so the day after tomorrow, I guess.'

Brant looked at Josie. 'How's that, eh? Wanna take a ride with me?'

Josie was pulling it back, spat, 'I've ridden worse.'

He was delighted. 'I believe you... do I ever!'

Back in the squad room, Nancy checked her desk for messages. Brant asked, 'Can I use the phone?'

'Sure.'

117

It took a time but eventually he was connected to Roberts. The squad room fell silent as Brant's London accent rang loud and entrancing. To them, he sounded *sooo* English.

'Guv, that you?'

'Yes.'

'It's Brant, I'm in New York.'

'And like it, do you?'

'I met with the Band-Aider, she's a piece of work.'

'Any problems?'

'Naw. What news of The Alien?'

Roberts knew he had to proceed carefully. He hedged, and as he did, a radio kicked into loud, sudden life with 'Don't Blame It On Me' by Stevie Nicks. Nancy went to turn it down.

Roberts said, 'Fenton's ex-wife has been murdered.'

Deep intake of breath, then Brant said, 'He bloody dun it... jeez!'

'Well, he's long gone, vanished without trace.'

'Yeah.'

'Falls went after that arsonist.'

'On her lonesome?'

'I'm afraid so.'

'Is she OK?'

Time to lie... 'Yes'.

A moment as Brant tasted the answer, decided it could suffice, then asked, 'Did you get the fuck?'

To the assembled detectives it sounded like — 'Did yah get the fok?' — and they loved it. In cop bars all over Manhattan, it had a brief shelf-life as the catch-phrase of the moment.

Roberts decided to play it a little humble and answered, '*We* got him.'

'Who, exactly?'

'Ahm... McDonald.'

Brant gave a bitter laugh. 'You'll get the credit, I suppose?'

118

Refute that.

Before Roberts knew how to answer, Brant said, 'Well, some of us have a job to do.'

And rang off.

Nancy took Brant to Choc Full O' Nuts. She asked for: 'Double decaffeinated latte,' and looked to Brant.

He said, 'Jaysus, I'd settle for a coffee.'

The waitress and Nancy exchanged a look that read: *'English… right!'* At least he hadn't asked for tea.

Brant reached for his best Hollywood accent, said, 'I'll need your shield and weapon.'

'What?'

'Gis a look.'

Suspicious, she took out the blue and gold shield.

He said, 'It looks like tin.'

'It is tin.'

'All we have is a warrant card… it doesn't quite have the same effect. Show me your weapon.' This with a leer.

She exclaimed, 'I can't figure you!'

'Don't bother. So, what are you carrying? Some dinky ·22 with a mother of pearl handle?' The coffee came and Brant stared at the double latte. 'Looks like cappuccino with an inflated ego.'

She took a sip, went, *'Mmmmm…* I carry a ·38.'

Brant had moved on, asked, 'What's yer full name?'

'Jesus H Christ, you jump all over the place. It's D'Agostino.'

He tasted the word then asked, 'Are you connected?'

'You're kidding.'

'What are ye calling it now… mob … family … crime syndicate?'

Nancy shook her head. The man was beyond help. She tried for a total shift, said, 'I have a list here, look… it's the places you'll probably want to see.'

The list:

119

Empire State
UN Building
Chrysler Building
Statue of Liberty
Macys.

He looked at it. 'What's this shit?'

'It's the sights.'

'Spare me the tourist crap. I want to see the Dakota building and the Chelsea Hotel.'

'Why?'

'Where John Lennon lived and then where Sid and
Nancy crashed. Plus, Bob Dylan wrote 'Sad-Eyed of the
Lowlands' in the Chelsea.'

Nancy was intrigued. 'Did you know they used the
Dakota in *Rosemary's Baby*?'

'Who gives a fuck?'

Nancy followed after him trying not to feel crushed,
when he suddenly turned. 'You know what the best sight
would be?'

'I have no idea.'

'You... without a stitch on.'

Nancy D'Agostino's husband had been killed in an auto
smash.

His bad luck.

Nancy had survived. She called that her bad luck.

The sole passion of Brant's life had been his Ed McBain
collection. He'd had the early green Penguin editions at 2/6
a throw. On through the author's outings as Evan Hunter
and the Matthew Hope series. Of the nigh eighty titles produced by McBain, he had close to the full collection.

For some reason, the police procedures struck a chord
with Brant. As if the boys of the 87th came closest to what in
his heart he believed a cop should be. When Nancy asked
him, 'Is there *anything* you value?' he nearly told her.

But the Band-Aiders – Josie and Sean O'Brien – had

120

broken into Brant's flat, trashed it and his book collection. Thus had begun his pursuit of them which ended in the death of a young policeman and Brant's own narrow escape.

It crossed Brant's mind that the whole story might get him a sympathetic fuck, but he decided to forego the telling.

For his last night in New York, Nancy had taken him to the restaurant on top of the World Trade Centre. On the elevator up, he'd bitched about the SMOKE FREE ZONE. As they were seated, Nancy said, 'Some view, huh?'

'Better through a nicotine haze.'

Nancy ordered seafood chowder and Brant ordered steak. Rare and bleeding.

Nancy said, 'That man you bumped into on the way in... it was Ed McBain.'

She couldn't believe his reaction, as if he'd had a prod in the ass. 'What? Are you serious? ... Oh *shit!* ... Is he gone?'

Like that.

When he finally calmed, he shook his head, muttering, 'Ed McBain... Jesus!'

Nancy took a sip of her Tom Collins. 'It was him or Elmore Leonard... I always get them crime writers confused.'

Brant was beyond comment; took out his Weights, lit one and exhaled: '*Ah...*'

Naturally, the Maitre d' came scurrying over but Nancy flashed the tin. He wasn't impressed. 'There are rules.'

Brant smiled and said, 'Hey pal, want to step outside and discuss procedure?'

He didn't.

After, they stood outside and Nancy wondered *what now*? Brant flagged a cab and held the door for her. Yet again, he'd taken her off balance. Manners were the very last thing she'd anticipated. He said to the cabbie, 'Take the lady home,' and they were peeling rubber. She looked back through the window to wave, or... But Brant was staring up at the World Trade.

Applicant

Bill was interviewing killers. Well, would-be or wanna-be ones. As usual, he held court in the end section of The Greyhound. Situated at The Oval, it's a bar that restores pride in the business, and for as long as Bill had been kingpin in south-east London, he'd treated it as his office.

What to look for in a potential hit man.

1. Patience
2. Cool
3. Absolute ruthlessness

A hard man who'd never have to shout the odds. You didn't ask about his rep, it had already reached you. Word was out that Fenton, The Alien, had lost it or gone to the US. Which amounted to the same thing if you clubbed in Clapham. (No, not night discos but crash-yer-skull clubs.)

Bill had already seen four guys. All young and all bananas. They wanted to be on the front page of the tabloids. Trainee psychos and apprentice sociopaths. They'd call attention. Sipping from a Ballygowan, Bill said to one of his minders, 'I miss the old days.'

'Guv?'

'Get the motor, we'll call it a day.'

'Call it what, Guv?'

He sighed. With the Russian villains making in-roads, maybe it was time to head for the Costa and listen to Phil Collins albums. Or album. Seeing how he simply recorded the same one each time.

The minder said, 'Guv, there's one other bloke.'

'Yeah?'

'That's him by the cider pump.'

Bill saw a guy in his early twenties, leather jacket, faded jeans, trainers. The urban uniform. There were half a million right outside the door. Nothing to distinguish him, which was a huge plus.

Bill said, 'Send him over.'

The guy moved easily, no wasted energy.

Bill nodded, said, 'Take a stool.'

'Yes, sir.'

Another plus. The last time Bill had heard 'sir' was in an Elvis interview. He offered a drink, got, 'No, sir.'

'Shit,' thought Bill. 'This kid could *surprise* a bloke to death.' He asked, 'You got a name, son?'

'Collie. It's Collie, sir.'

'What, cos you like dogs, is it?' And got to see the kid's eyes. Dark eyes that were ever so slightly out of alignment. They gave the sense of relief that you weren't their focus. Nor would you ever want to be.

Now the kid smiled, almost shyly. 'Something that happened when I was young.'

Bill smiled, like the kid had to be all of twenty three. 'Tell me.' Not a request.

'Our neighbour had a dog; every time you passed he threw himself against the gate. People got a fright regular as clockwork. Like, one minute there wasn't a sign of him, then as you passed, he'd jump snarling and barking.' Bill didn't comment, so the kid continued. 'The dog got off on it.'

'What?'

'Yes, he got his jollies from it.' He pronounced the word 'yollies', giving it a resonance of distance and disease.

Bill had to ask – 'How did you know that?'

Now the kid gave a shrug, said, 'I looked into his eyes.'

'Oh.'

'Yeah, before I strangled him, I took a good look.'

123

Bill decided to ask the important question. 'What is it you want, son?'

'To work for you, sir.'

'And what do you want, to be famous, get yourself a rep?'

Now the kid looked irritated, said, 'I'm not stupid, sir.'

'Done time, 'ave you?'

'Once. I won't be going back.'

Bill believed him. 'OK... I'll give you a trial.' Now he reached in his jacket, took out a black and white photo, pushed it across the table. 'Know him?'

'No, sir.'

It showed Brant, resplendent in his Aran sweater as he boarded a flight. His face to the camera, he looked like he hadn't a care in the world. Bill stared at it for a while then, back to biz, said, 'That's Detective Sergeant Brant. Due back from America any day.' The kid waited. 'Your predecessor, The Alien, was supposed to put some pressure on the man, persuade him to drop his interest in me. But... he fucked it up. And Brant not only *didn't* lose interest, he paid me a visit.' Bill's face was bright red. Famous for his cool, he was close to losing it. 'What I want is to hit him where it hurts. Not *him* – too much attention if he's damaged personally. But if something he cared for got nobbled...' He stopped, asked, 'Do you follow me, son?'

'Yes, sir. Damage where he'll feel it.'

'That's it. Think you can handle it?'

'Yes, sir.'

Bill reached again in his pocket, took out a thin wedge. It had the glow of fifties. He nudged it across the table. 'To get you started; a bit of walking round money.'

The kid didn't touch it. 'I haven't earned it yet.'

'That's what you think.'

124

Something in the way she moves

Falls finally crashed through the surface and immediately wished she hadn't. As soon as she opened her eyes she knew the baby was gone.

Then the event of the pool hall returned and her whole body shook. She knew if she called, a gaggle of help would arrive. Instead, she cried silently… and as the tears coursed down her face she remembered the fourth Teletubby.

Po.

The very name raised her to new heights of anguish. Finally, she stirred and sat up. Looking down to the IV, she tore it from her arm and pulled the needle from the monitor. A wave of nausea engulfed her, but she weathered it. Got her feet on the floor and felt the room heave.

A nurse came rushing. 'What on earth are you doing?'

Falls slowly raised her head and tried to focus. She gave a sad bitter laugh, answered, 'Now, isn't that a good question?'

At almost the same time, an impromptu party had begun in the police canteen. Roberts was being toasted with beer and cider.

The duty sergeant raised a glass. 'Let's hear it for DI Roberts… hip, hip!'

Roberts acknowledged the toast and then indicated McDonald. 'I had help.'

More cheers. More booze.

The Super dropped in for a moment, gave Roberts a gruff nod. 'Well done, laddie.' Which was rich, him being five years younger. As these events go, it was tame – muted, even – due to Falls still being in hospital.

The duty sergeant, by way of conversation, said to Roberts, 'You'll 'ave heard about the new Mickey Finn the buggers are using?'

He hadn't, said, 'I haven't.'

'Aye, they meet a young girl in the pub or a club and buy her a drink, slip Rohypnol into it and the poor lass blacks out. Comes to next day after five of them have raped her.'

'Jesus!'

'Aye, that too.'

Roberts wondered if anything like that had happened with his daughter. Fear and rage crept along his spine. Finishing a pale ale, he resolved to turn everything round. He'd go home, say to the missus, 'Listen honey, let's have a fresh start. I have skin cancer, I'm skint too (a little humour), and let's talk about our daughter. Who banged her up?' It would need work but it was nearly there. He had the drive home to polish it…

With his career now having a shot of adrenalin, he felt downright optimistic. Parked the car and stood for a moment outside his house, thought: 'OK, we're mortgaged to the bloody hilt but we've still got it. Hell, *I've* still got it.'

Thus emboldened, he went in, shouted, 'Yo… I'm home.'

No answer.

Never-no-mind – he'd grab a bite from the kitchen and begin the new life. He began to hum the truly horrendous 'Begin The Beguine'. He hummed mainly cos he didn't know the words. Opened the fridge. It was bare, like, completely empty, save for a note taped to a sorry lump of cheese. He read:

'WE'VE GONE TO MY MOTHER'S. THAT'S IF YOU EVER GET HOME TO NOTICE'.

That was it.

He held on to the handle of the fridge, then muttered, 'Now, that's one cold note.'

Montezuma's Revenge

The Alien admired his growing tan, thought: *Yah handsome devil!*

The thing about foreign holidays was you could do all the asshole things you'd always ridiculed. Such as:

1. Wear Bermudas
2. Perch shades on yer hair
3. Carry a bum bag

Reg Fenton was many things – ruthless, determined, and uncompromising. What he had never been was given to flights of fancy. He had no truck with superstitions, omens, any of that. He believed in what was in front of him. Sitting at the bar, he was drinking tequila with all the trimmings. Salt on the hand, slices of lemon and sure, it gave the rush. He suspected all the ritual was a crock, but what the hell. He said originally…. 'When in Mex!'

A tape was playing Dire Straits' 'Ticket to Heaven'. A song that proves, yeah, them guys did have something. Glancing out the window, he saw Stella and dropped his glass. The waiter, startled: 'Que pasa?'

Fenton looked at him, then back to the window, she was gone. He moved to the waiter, grabbed his arm, shouted, 'Did you see her…? Jesus H Christ… it was her!'

'No comprende, Senor!'

Fenton let him go, tried to rein in his emotions, then staggered over to a table and sat heavily. The waiter approached, nervous as a rat. 'Senor would like something?'

'Yeah, get outta my face, arsewipe… no… hey… get me a tequila. Shit, bring the whole bottle.'

As the waiter got this from the bar, he put his finger to his forehead, made circular motions, whispered, 'Mucho loco.'

The barman nodded. Tourists, gringos, Americanos… he'd seen all their shit.

I have a need

Demian in 'Exorcist III'

ollie was euphoric. He felt the wedge of cash in his
hip pocket and thought: *I'm on my way…* To step right
into the big time. But he'd need to get heeled, get a
shooter. On the Isle of Wight, he'd celled with a Yardie, one of
the Jamaican gangs who terrorised North London. His name
was Jamal. Out now, he kept a low profile and kept it in
Brixton; the busy end of Railton Road. He had the bottom
half of a terraced house. Upstairs was a fortune teller. Collie
could smell the weed halfway down the street. He knocked
three times like the horrendous song from the seventies.

A white woman answered, aged about thirty. Her eyes
were lost, but she had an attitude. 'What?'

'Tell Jamal it's Collie.'

A black arm reached out and pulled her aside. Jamal,
bare chested, gave a golden tooth grin. 'Me mon!'
Which is like 'Hi' … sorta.

He gave Collie a hug and then they did the series of high-
fives and palm slapping.

Buddy stuff.

Inside, Dubstar were laying down a cloud and Jamal
said, 'Yo bitch, y'all git some tea fo' my bro.' He gave
another illuminating smile. 'She from rich white folk.'

'Yeah?'

'Yeah, de bitch be into Marxism and Jamal be in ho ass
and trust fund.'

'How'd you find her?'

130

'She be sellin' de *Big Issue*... I bought de lot, bought ho back mo crib. That be Tuesday... what day is dis, mon?'

'Ahm... Tuesday.'

Jamal looked perplexed, then said, 'Must be some other Tuesday. So, bro, wanna *Big Issue*?'

And they laughed together. Just two bros, hanging in the hood.

The woman brought mint tea in glasses and four cakes on a brass tray. Jamal said, 'De tea be Julep like de cats in Marrakesh and de cakes be hash brownies... mo hash than cake... yo cool?'

He was.

In addition, Jamal rolled the Camberwell Carrot made famous by *Withnail And I*. Jamal had an added ingredient: he lightly sprinkled angel dust on the paper. It didn't quite blast yer head off but it sure put you in orbit.

As Collie felt the countdown to oblivion he forced himself to concentrate on biz. 'I need something.'

'Sure, mon, whatcha be needin'?'

'A shooter.'

'My mon, I no do dat sheet no mo.'

Collie waited, skipped his turn on the tote, nibbled on a cake. Finally, Jamal said, 'Less I gives mo own piece... mah personal protection. How dat be?'

'I'd hate to leave you... defenceless.'

Big Jamal grin. 'Sheet, I git by somehows.' He stood up, said, 'Gis a mo.'

'Sure.'

The woman hunched down on the floor, lotus style. Collie could see her knickers, and more, he could see she saw. Then she raised a brownie to her mouth began to nibble...

gnaw ... gnaw ... gnaw.

She asked, 'See something you like?'

'Nope.'

'Are you queer?'

131

The dust was popping along his brain and tiny colours were exploding on the edge of his vision. He didn't answer, tried to focus on the brightness. In Stephen King's novel *It*, the clown says, 'Come into my bright lights'. Then it shows rotten razored teeth. Collie looked at the woman, half expecting her to do likewise.

The trance was broken by the return of Jamal. He carried an oil clothed bundle, sat and unravelled it. A gleaming gun slid onto the table. Collie whistled. 'A bloody cannon.'

Jamal gave the big grin. 'It's a Ruger six speed, see what's on de barrel there?'

It read 'Magnum'.

Jamal put a closed fist down alongside the gun, said, 'Here de icing on de cake!' And opened his hand. Six dum dum bullets rolled out. 'They puts a fat hole in de target.'

'How much?' Jamal held up five fingers. Collie shook his head. For the next ten minutes they haggled, giggled, fingered. Eventually, they settled on three. The dope had kicked in and with full ferocity. It took Collie ages to count out the price, but finally it got done.

The woman glared at them. If dope is meant to mellow you, no one had told her. And she was sufficiently out of it not to disguise her aversion. Collie looked at her, then laid a five spot on the pile. 'Buy sweets for the child.' Set them off again.

Jamal pulled his zipper down, said, 'Git some o dis mama.' She didn't move so he added, 'I ain't *axin* you, bitch.' He picked up the Ruger, put a dum dum in.

Collie said, 'Hey Jam... don't handle *my* weapon!'

They were off again, huge hilarity. Just ebony and ivory crackin' up, having a walk on the wild side. The woman approached, hunkered down and took Jamal in her mouth. Collie closed his eyes. This he didn't need to see. Loud groans followed.

'*Sheeet, arghh... fuck it...*'

When Collie opened his eyes, Jamal said, 'I need a cigarette.'

132

The woman was wiping her mouth, a brightness in her eyes as if to say: *Top that.*

Collie got to his feet, said, or tried to say: 'Time to rock 'n' roll.'

Jamal asked, 'Yo bro, ya wans a BJ?'

Collie looked at the woman who was now smirking. 'Thanks, but I already ate.'

Jamal's laughter followed him out into the street.

Collie had tucked the gun in the waistband of his jeans. At the back, of course.

Fist

'How d'ya feel about blood sports?'

McDonald was taken aback by Roberts' question. He'd earned some kudos, he didn't want to blow them. 'You mean like coursing, fox hunting?'

'No, I mean pugilism.'

'Ahm…'

'It's bare fisted boxing, like Harry S Corbett, Diamond Jim… There's a bout at The Elephant tonight.'

'And we're going to bust 'em?'

Roberts laughed, said 'There'll be over two hundred punters gathered. Hard asses. We're going to have a wager.'

'But Guv – isn't it illegal?'

'Course it is, why d'ya think it's exciting?'

As Roberts predicted, there were at least two hundred gathered. All men, and as per, the very air bristled with unspoken aggression and excitement. The 'bout' was to take place at the sheltered car park to the rear of the Elephant.

When they got there, Roberts said, 'Back in a mo.'

McDonald was wearing a black leather jacket and jeans, felt he smelt of cop.

A punter said, 'Wanna drink, John?'

And offered a flask.

'Sure.' Best to blend. He took a swig and near choked, felt molten lava run down his throat, burning all in its path. He gasped, asked, '*What… was… that*?'

'Surg and chicken soup.' Surg as in surgical spirits. The

134

infamous White Lady of south-east London drinking schools. He could only hope to fuck that the guy was kidding.

When Roberts returned, he collided with a young guy. There was a moment it hung there, then Roberts said, 'Excuse me.' And Collie nodded.

The fighters emerged to a mix of cheers, catcalls, whistles. Roberts said, 'The big guy, he's from Liverpool and evens favourite. The other is a London boy.'

Both men were bare-chested, wearing only shorts and trainers. No frills. The London boy was runtish but he had a wiry look. In contrast, the Liverpudlian was a brick shithouse. His muscles had muscle and he exuded confidence.

Roberts said, 'Best get yer wager on.'

'What?'

'Don't tell me you're not going to have a go.'

'Oh… right… ahm.'

'See the guy in the black suit? He's the bookie.'

'OK… how much… I mean… would five be enough?'

Roberts scoffed, 'Don't be so Scottish… have a decent go. I've already dun Liverpool, so you take "the boy".'

'But he's the underdog.'

'All the better. Hurry up, now.'

A bell sounded and the bout began. Each round was approximately five minutes but it wasn't rigid – the third round lasted ten.

McDonald had grown up in Glasgow and as a copper he was accustomed to violence. But this spectacle sickened him. It was the crunch of bare knuckles on bone. Real and stereophonic. He asked, 'What are the rules?'

'There aren't… sometimes biting isn't allowed.'

'*Sometimes?*'

'Shut up and watch… I think your boy's in trouble.'

He was.

Bleeding from his eye and mouth, he looked for escape. None available.

Then all of a sudden he seemed to be electric, and head-butted Lou. who staggered back. Like a terrier, the boy went after him, and with three blows to the head, Lou was down.

The boy walked round him then kicked him in the back of the head.

All she wrote.

McDonald said, 'I won!'

Roberts said, '*We* won.'

'I thought you backed the favourite?'

'Yeah... for *us*. Like you did... for *us*. Hurry up before yer bookie legs it.'

When McDonald collected his winnings he half considered legging it himself. Reluctantly, he handed a wedge to Roberts who said, 'Lucky I made you get a bet on eh?'

'Yeah... lucky.'

In the pub, Roberts said, 'Get 'em in, lad, nobody likes a tight-fisted winner. I'll have a brandy.'

When McDonald had followed the Morse series on TV, he'd felt it was unreal. Now he was reconsidering. Roberts took his drink and asked, 'What's that you're drinking?'

'Snakebite.'

'Eh?'

'It's lager and white cider.'

'Time to grow up son... get us a couple of scotches, eh?'

I had a dream

(ABBA)

When Falls was discharged from hospital, it was AHA – not the Scandinavian pop group, but Against Hospital Advice. Like she could care.

The doctor said, 'Would you consider counselling?'

'Which would do what for me exactly?'

'Ahm... help you get over your... trauma.'

'I lost my baby, it's not a trauma... and no, I don't want to "get over" that. And I don't expect to.'

The doctor, flustered, said, 'I've taken the liberty of pre-scribing some medication... I...'

'No thanks.'

'Might I suggest you reconsider?'

'No.'

Falls took a cab home. The driver droned on about a range of topics. She neither heard nor answered him as they drove along Balham High Road. She said, 'Here... drop me here.'

The driver saw the off licence and thought *Uh-oh*, said: 'Mother's little helper, eh?'

The words lashed her but she managed to keep control and asked, 'How much?' She fumbled a rush of coins and pushed them at him.

Like his brethren, he wasn't to be hurried. 'You've given me too much, darlin'.'

'Alas, the same can't be said for you.'

But he'd triggered something and she bought a bottle of gin. The sales assistant asked, 'A mixer?'

'No thanks.'

She thought gin 'n' pain would mix enough. Her father hadn't drank gin. He drank everything else, including water from the toilet bowl, but alcoholically maintained: 'Gin makes me ill'.

He drank for no reason.

She had a reason.

Perhaps she'd uncovered a dual motive.

Entering her home was nigh unbearable. In her wardrobe were the baby things. She got a cup from the kitchen, sat, uncapped the bottle and poured. Said: 'Here's to Po,' and drank.

Two hours later she put the baby stuff in the garbage.

The following morning she was as sick as a dog, but she dragged herself to the shower and readied her energies, knowing she was going to need them.

Arriving at the station, the desk sergeant exclaimed, 'Good God!' Then tried for composure. What was he to offer – sympathy, encouragement… what? He did the procedural thing – he passed the buck. 'I'll let the Super know you're here… ahm… take a seat.'

Like Joe Public.

Various colleagues passed and seemed embarrassed. No one knew how to respond.

The Sergeant said, 'The Super will see you now.' He gave a dog smile as if he'd done a good turn. She felt her stomach somersault.

She wasn't invited to sit by the Super. He asked, 'How are you doing?'

'Not too bad, sir, fit for duty.'

He frowned, looked down at his hands, then, 'Perhaps it would be best if you took some time… the criminals will still be here, eh?'

He gave a police manual laugh. This has absolutely no relation to humour. Rather, it's the signal for shafting. Falls waited and eventually he said, 'Take a month, eh? Catch up on the ironing.'

Even he realised this was hardly PC, but she answered, 'Thank you, sir, but I'd like to get back.'

Now he cleared his throat. 'I'm afraid that won't be possible... there may be an enquiry.'

Falls was astonished. 'Why?'

'There's a question of... recklessness... Going after a villain alone... the powers that be...' (here he paused to let her know: *hey, this is not* my *idea*), 'frown on... mavericks.'

She was going to argue but knew it was useless.

He said, 'You're suspended on half-pay pending an enquiry.'

She considered for only a moment, then said, 'I don't think so.'

'I beg your pardon?'

'I resign.'

'I don't think...'

She got out her warrant card, laid it on the desk and turned to go.

He blustered, 'I'm not quite through WPC.'

And she gave a tiny smile. 'But I am... all through.'

Twenty minutes later she was home with a fresh bottle of gin.

No mixer.

Taming the Alien

Fenton could hear Celine Dion with 'You Are The Reason' and wasn't sure was it real or a memory.

He stared intently at the almost empty tequila bottle. No worm at the bottom.

The Alien had followed Stella into the poor part of town. At least he thought it was her. He'd yet to catch up on her, see her full face. She was always an elusive ten yards away. Gradually, he'd been lured into the shanty area. All the evidence of dire poverty escaped him. Spotting the sign 'CANTINA', he'd stumbled into a shack. Now he shouted to the bartender, 'Where's my worm?'

'Que?'

'I can't see him! Jesus… unless I ate the fucker… Can yah eat them?'

The barman shrugged his shoulders. He was about to close as the wind was up and howling. The Alien had a mess of dollars before him. The barman pocketed them, shoved a bottle of mescal into Fenton's arms then got him outside. 'Go, Senor, the hurricane ees here.'

'Fuck off.'

Fenton slumped down against the shack, opened the mescal, drank deep and shuddered. Then he closed his eyes.

✝

When the hurricane hit, the poorer areas took the brunt.

The tourist hotels, resort and apartments escaped.

Down in the shanty the Cantina was practically demolished.

It took a long time for the rescue teams to find Fenton, and by the time they got him to hospital, it was too late to save his legs.

Run for home

(Lindisfarne)

Brant was finishing his first doughnut. A second, heavily sugared, sat expectant.

Nancy said, 'I hate to rush you.'

'You won't, don't worry.'

She looked at her watch. 'You wouldn't want to be late.'

He bit into the remaining cake and Nancy added, 'You'd slide right into the NYPD.'

'Think so?'

Nervously, she produced a package. 'It's for you.'

'A present?'

'Well, to remind you of your trip.'

'This travel lark is a blast – people keep giving me stuff.'

Without finesse, he tore open the package. Inside was a Macys tag and a hat. He said, 'It's a hat.'

'Like Popeye Doyle.'

'Who?'

'In the movie 'French Connection'

Then she saw him laughing and she blustered, 'I didn't know what you'd wear – a fedora, a Trilby, a derby…?'

'But you knew I'd wear it well.'

For one awful moment she thought he was going to sing.

He stood up, said, 'I hate to rush you.'

As they drove to Kennedy, she didn't know whether she would be relieved or sad at his going.

Brant thought: 'The hat'll be a nice surprise for Roberts…'

A room had been set aside for the transfer of the prisoner. As Brant and Nancy waited, he signed the ton of paperwork. Then he took out his Weights and checked the wall. Yup, right there: SMOKE FREE ZONE.

He lit up. Nancy ignored him.

As he fingered the Zippo, he suddenly acted on impulse, said, 'Here, it was my Dad's.'

Nancy looked at the offered lighter, said 'Oh, I couldn't.'

'OK.' And he put it back in his pocket.

The door opened and Josie was let through. In chains. A belt round her waist joined manacles from her wrists to her ankles. Naturally, it impeded movement and she had to shuffle pigeon-toed. Four guards with her. Brant said, 'For fucksake!'

Josie gave a rueful smile, said, 'I'll never get through the metal detector.'

As the handover was done, all the chains were removed and then a new long handcuff was placed on her right wrist, the other cuff offered to Brant.

Before he could respond, Nancy said, 'It's regulations.'

'It's bloody nonsense.'

But he took the cuff. Josie said, 'Like we're engaged.'

Nancy said, 'We accompany you to the aircraft, then it's all your show.'

They were boarded before the other passengers and right at the rear of the plane. Two rows ahead would be kept empty.

Nancy said, 'You better not smoke.'

'Me?'

The guards left and Nancy had a word with the Chief Steward, then she stood before Brant. 'I guess it's been fun.'

'Don't let me keep you, D'Agostino.'

She turned and was half way down the aisle when he shouted, 'Yer a good un, Nance.'

Not sure what that meant, she decided it was complimentary, and hugged it thus.

143

Josie asked, 'Did yah ride her?'

'Watch yer lip.'

Brant reached over, unlocked the cuffs. She massaged her wrist. 'Thanks.'

'Any messin', I'll break yer nose, OK?'

Josie gave him a long look. 'I could give you a blow job.'

He laughed in spite of himself. What was amazing to him was she was kind of likable. In a twisted, selfish fashion, he felt almost protective. He tried to dissipate that with: 'You'll get some reception in prison – you being a police killer.'

She nodded. 'Least I'll get a decent cup o' tea.'

'You'll get a hell of a lot more than tea, me girl.'

She looked out the window. 'I'm afraid.'

'You have good reason, lass.'

'No, I mean… of flying.'

Brant nearly laughed again, said

'Jaysus, you'd be better off if we crashed.'

'Can I hold yer hand for take-off?'

Brant shook his head and then she left a piece of paper on his knee. He asked, 'What?' And uncrumbled it to find a five dollar bill. Soiled, worn, torn, but hanging in there.

She said, 'I'll buy the drinks.'

'How did you hide it?'

She gave a slow smile. 'Them yanks isn't all they're cracked up to be.'

As the plane took off, he saw the sweat on her forehead. He placed his hand on hers and she nodded.

Once airborne, the hostess asked, 'Like a drink? It has to be a soft one for your… companion.'

'A Coke for her and two large Bacardis.'

'Ahm…'

Brant stared at her, defying her to question him. She let it go. Josie said nothing.

When the drinks came, he measured them evenly and indicated Josie to take one. She said, 'I love rum 'n' coke.'

'Well drink it then.'

She did.

The in-flight movie commenced and Josie said, 'I love the pictures.'

Shooting

Collie watched the funeral with a sense of awe. All the taxi drivers of south-east London had turned out for their murdered colleague. Each cab had a black ribbon tied to its antennae and they fluttered in the light breeze.

'*I* caused this. They're here cos of *me*.'

It was a heady sensation. Collie had figured he needed a dry run with the gun, to see if he had the balls. He did.

Kept it lethal and simple. Hailed a cab at The Oval, blew the guy's head off at Stockwell. Then walked away. He couldn't believe the rush. He hadn't touched the takings – he was a professional, not a bloody thief.

The few days previous, he'd done his Brant research. All that required was hanging in the cop pubs. To say they were loose tongued was to put it mildly – numerous times he heard of Brant travelling home with a woman. Next he rang the station and, in his best TV voice said, 'This is Chief Inspector Ryan of Serious Crimes at the Yard. We need the assistance of Sergeant Brant.'

Mention of the Yard did all the work. He was told the time and terminal of arrival. Now, on the day, he put on a black suit and dog collar, checked himself in the mirror and said, 'Reverend....? You looking at me?'

At The Oval, he bought a ticket for Heathrow and *The Big Issue* to pass the journey. As he settled into his seat, the gun was only slightly uncomfortable in the small of his back.

A woman offered him a piece of chocolate and he said, 'God bless you my child.'

At the airport, he checked the arrivals board and settled down to wait.

Over Heathrow, the plane was preparing to land. Brant said, 'We've got to cuff up.'

'I like bin chained to yah.'

'Jaysus, girl!'

Then she lowered her head. 'I'm sorry. '

'What?'

'For yer trouble.'

'Yeah…well…'

In truth, he didn't know what to say. Being sorry hardly cut it, but… He said, 'Leastways you'll get a decent cup o' tea.'

'Two sugars?'

'Sure, why not?'

As Brant and Josie emerged into arrivals, he slung his jacket to hide the cuff. Collie saw them and thought: *Holding hands. How sweet.*

He moved up to the barrier, Brant vaguely clocked a priest and looked away. The gun was out and Collie put two rounds in Josie's chest. The impact threw her back, pulling Brant along. Collie was moving fast and away, the gun back in his waistband.

Brant leant over Josie, saw the holes pumped by the dum dums and shouted, 'Oh God!'

Collie was at the taxi rank and his collar allowed him to jump the queue. That, plus cheek.

'Central London,' he said.

His elation and adrenalin was clouded by what he'd seen. A handcuff? How could that be?

Then he realised the driver was talking… incessantly. Collie touched the gun and smiled.

147

Acts ending –
if not concluding

When Bill heard of the airport shooting he shouted 'What the bloody blue fuck is the matter with everyone? Can't anybody do a blasted thing right?'

His minder didn't know, said, 'I dunno.'

'Course you don't bloody know, yah thick fuck.'

What Bill knew was the shit was about to hit the fan – and hard.

He headed home and his daughter Chelsea was waiting. She said, 'I love you, Dad.'

Bill had recently caught a BBC documentary on Down's syndrome. The children had been titled 'the gentle prophets'. He wasn't entirely sure what it meant but he liked it.

Picking up Chelsea, he asked, 'Want to go on a trip with yer Dad?'

'Oh yes!'

'Good girl.'

'Where, Dad?'

'Somewhere far and till things cool off.'

'Can we go tomorrow Dad?'

'Darlin', we're going today.'

✝

Roberts was once again before the Super. A very agitated Super, who asked, 'What the bloody hell is going on?'

'Sir?'

'Don't "sir" me, Roberts... the fiasco at the airport... Who on earth would shoot the woman?'

'They say it was a priest.'

The Super displayed a rare moment of wit, said 'Lapsed Catholic, was she?'

Roberts gave the polite smile, about one inch wide.

The Super snapped, 'It's hardly a joking matter! Could it have been Brant he was after?'

'It seems to have been a very definite hit, sir.'

'Where's Brant now?'

'Still at Heathrow – Special Branch are de-briefing him.'

The Super stood up, began pacing. Not a good sign. He was muttering, 'God only knows what the Yanks will make of this.'

A knock at the door and a woman looked in. 'Ready for your tea, and biccy, sir?'

He exploded, 'Tea? I don't want bloody tea, I want results!'

She fled.

The Super leant on the desk. 'You'll have to have a word with WPC Fell.'

'Falls, sir.'

'What, like the present continuous of the verb 'to fall', not the past tense? You're giving me an English lesson?'

'No, sir... I...'

'The damn woman has resigned. I mean, her being black... you know... *Minority Policing* and all that horse-shit... Get her back.' Before Roberts could reply, the Super was off again, 'Well don't hang about, eh?'

'Yes, sir.'

Roberts had reached the door when the Super said, 'Send in me tea.'

Brief debriefing

W e'd like you to go through it one more time, Sergeant.'

Brant lit up a Weight, took a deep drag, exhaled. 'You're trying to learn it by heart, that it?'

The two men conducting the interview wore suits. One had a black worsted, the other a tweed Oxford. Black said, patiently, 'There may be some detail you've forgotten.'

'It's on tape, yer mate in the Oxfam job had a recorder.'

Oxford said, 'We're anxious to let you get home.'

Brant sat back, said, 'We arrived at Heathrow, I re-cuff us–'

'Re-cuff?'

'Is there an echo?'

'Let me understand this, Sergeant. The woman was *uncuffed* during the flight?'

'You catch on quick, boyo.'

The men exchanged a glance, then: 'Please continue.'

'We got off the plane and I covered the cuffs with me jacket…'

Another exchanged look.

'Then we came out and a priest shot her.'

'What makes you think he was a priest?'

'Was he was a good shot? What d'ya think, he looked like Bing Crosby?'

Now Oxford allowed his skepticism to show, said 'He was hardly a priest.'

'Are you catholic?'

'No, but I hardly see…'

'If you were a catholic, you'd not be surprised what priests are capable of.'

Black decided to take control – cut the shit, cut to the chase. '*You* won't be shedding any tears, will you Sergeant?'

'What's that mean?'

'Well, I mean… like someone did you a favour, eh? She tried to murder you once, killed one of your colleagues… how much can you be hurting?'

Brant was up. 'Enough of this charade, I'm off.'

Oxford moved to block the door and Brant smiled. ''Scuse me.'

Oxford stepped aside. Brant opened the door, paused, said: 'I may need to talk to you two again. Don't leave town.'

J is for Judgement

(Sue Grafton)

Roberts met with Brant in The Cricketers. He'd parked his car near The Oval, said to *The Big Issue* vendor, 'Keep an eye, eh?' and indicated the motor.

The vendor said, 'Play fair, Guv, they'd steal yer eye.'

Brant was at the back of the pub, a tepid coffee before him. Roberts put out his hand. 'Good to see you, Tom,' and meant it. Then, 'Don't you want a real drink?'

'With all me soul but I was afraid to start.'

'Start now.'

'I will.'

They did. Whiskey chasers.

No conversation, let the scotch fill the spaces. Then Brant rummaged in his jacket and produced a squashed hat, said, 'Got yah a present.'

'Oh.'

'It's a bit battered. I fell on it.'

Roberts tentatively touched it, then took it in both hands. 'I dunno what to say.'

'Give it some time, it will bounce back.'

'Like us, eh?'

Brant gave him a look as if he were only now really seeing him, asked, 'You were sick?'

At last thought Roberts, I can finally share. 'Naw, nothing worth mentioning.' Then he added, 'Falls is out.'

'Out where?'

'The force, she resigned.'

Brant was animated, life returning. 'She can't do that!'

'Word is you lent her the dosh to bury her father.'

'*Me*?'

'Did yah?'

'C'mon Guv, am I a soft touch?'

'What d'ya say we finish up, go round to see her?'

'Like now?'

'You have other plans?'

'Naw.'

They finished their drinks, got ready to go. Brant asked, 'Out of vague interest, how much am I supposed to have given her?'

'Two large.'

Brant didn't answer, just gave a low whistle. The figure was twice that, but then…

Who was counting?

In Balham, as they approached Falls' home, Roberts asked, 'How d'ya want to play this?'

'Let's make it up as we go along.'

'Good plan.'

They banged on the door and no reply. Roberts said, 'Could be she's out.'

'Naw, she's home, there's a light.' Brant took out his keys, said, 'Pretend you don't see this,' and he fidgeted with the lock, pushed the door in.

They were cops accustomed to nigh on any reception. Neither of them could have forecast a skinhead. All of fourteen years old and wielding an iron bar. He shouted, 'Fuck off outta it.'

'*Wot?*' in chorus.

The skin made a swipe with the bar, said: 'I'll do ye.'

Brant turned his back shrugged, then spun back, clouting the skin on the side of the skull. Flipped him, knelt on his back, said, 'What's yer game, laddie? Where's the woman?'

153

'Play fair, mate… jeez!'

Roberts had gone searching, shouted, 'She's here… in the bathroom.'

'Is she OK?'

'Debatable.'

Brant stood up, put a lock on the skin's neck, gave him two open-handed slaps. 'Whatcha do to her?'

'Didn't do nuffink! I'm protecting her!'

'*Wot*?' Again, in chorus.

Now the skin went bright red with a glow of injured dignity. 'She gave me a quid one time, so when I seen her 'elpless like, staggerin' home, leavin' the door open, I said I'd mind her till she got her act back. Know what I mean?'

They did, sorta.

Roberts took out his wallet, said 'Yah did good, now here's somefin for yer trouble.'

'I don't need paying… she's like… a mate.'

Brant looked at Roberts, then. 'All right, then, you ever get in a spot o' bother ask for DI Roberts or DS Brant, we'll see you right…OK?'

'OK.'

'Take off then, that's a good lad.'

He did.

Roberts said, 'I've seen it all, a skin protecting a copper.'

'A black copper.'

'Yeah… go figure.'

They couldn't.

Together they hoisted Falls into the shower, kept her there till she came round. She came to, to retch, to curse and struggle. Then they dried her and got her into a dressing gown.

Brant rooted in his wallet, took out two pills and forced them into Falls mouth. Roberts raised an eyebrow and Brant said, 'Tranqs… heavy duty sedation.'

Falls said, 'Don't want help.'

'Too bad – it's underway.'

Brant and Roberts took it in shifts over the next 48 hours, washing her, feeding her, holding her. Times they got some chicken soup down her, times she threw up all over them.

When the horrors came, as come they do, Brant held her tight, wiped the spittle from her mouth. When the sweats coursed down her body, Roberts changed the bed linen, got her a fresh T-shirt.

DAY 3:

Brant's shift. Falls had slept for eight hours. She woke, her eyes focused, asked, 'Can I have a cup of tea?'

'Toast?'

'OK… I think.'

She could. Two slices, lightly marged. Then she got outta bed, didn't stagger, said, 'I could murder a large gin.'

'Darlin', it's near murdered you.'

'I know… and yet…?'

Brant went and found a drop in one of the pile of bottles, said, 'There's a taste in this, enough to fuel you to the off licence.' He held out the drink. 'What's it gonna be, darlin'?'

Perspiration lined her forehead, a tremor hit her body, she said, 'I ache for it.'

He didn't speak.

Then she shut her eyes, tight like a child before a surprise. 'Sling it.'

He did.

Later, after another shower, she asked, 'Why?'

'Why what?'

'You and the Guv… helped me.'

'Well, they say you owe me three large, I'm protecting me cash.'

'I've resigned.'

Brant stood up, said, 'Don't be stupid, I'll see you at the station. Be on time, WPC.'

'Which party would you like
to be invited to?'
'The one', I said, 'least
likely to involve gunfire.'

('Midnight In The Garden Of Good and
Evil' – John Berendt)

Collie was having a party for one. It's not difficult to prepare such an event. You buy enough booze for six and don't invite anyone. He'd laid out on his coffee table:

4 Bottles of Wild Turkey
2 Six Packs of Bud.
1 Cheese Dip and
The gun.

The gun isn't always a prerequisite, it depends who's after you.

Music.

Verve with 'Lucky Man', over and over.

To complete the festivities, he'd put down four lines of coke.

Ready to party.

When the phone rang, he picked up the receiver, breathed, 'Yeah?' Lots of muscle in it.

A pause at the other end, then, 'So you're home.'

Collie recognised Bill straight off, answered, 'Yes, sir.'

'You screwed up.'

156

'Wasn't my fault, sir, I thought she was his bit of gear.'

'Didn't the handcuffs signify something else?'

'I didn't see them, sir... I thought they was holding hands... I can fix it, though.'

'How?'

'I'll do Brant.'

'And you call that fixing it?'

'I dunno, sir... tell me and I'll do it... I done the taxi driver good, didn't I?'

A long pause, a sigh, then: 'You did the taxi driver?'

'Yes, sir, one shot, clean as anything.'

'OK. Stay home, don't go out... Can you do that?'

'Yes, sir.'

'Good.'

✝

When Brant got home, there was an envelope under his door. No stamp. Inside was a single sheet of paper. It read:

'THE AIRPORT SHOOTER LIVES AT:

FLAT 4, 102 VINE STREET,

CLAPHAM JUNCTION.'

Brant picked up the phone, dialled, then heard Falls say, 'Hello?'

'It's Brant. Wanna be a hero?'

✝

There's a hospital on the outskirts of Acapulco called La Madonna D'Esperanza.

The Virgin of Hope.

It's a mental hospital, and hope is pretty scarce.

Pan along Corridor C, turn left towards the windows and there's a man in a wheelchair. He's silent because he's learnt she won't appear if he speaks. His hands rest on the rug covering his lower torso.

157

If he keeps his eyes glued to the panes, she'll eventually come, and then he'll whisper:

Stell.

Stella.

Ken Bruen

hails from the west of Ireland and divides his time between Galway and south London. His past includes drunken brawls in Vietnam, a stretch of four months in a South American gaol, a PhD in metaphysics and four of the most acclaimed crime novels of the decade.

Taming The Alien is the second in his landmark WHITE TRILOGY, following on from *A White Arrest*.